DIARY OF A
HOMELESS
PRODIGAL

DIARY OF A HOMELESS PRODIGAL

Obi B. Egbuna

Fourth Dimension Publishing Co., Ltd.

First Published 1976 by
FOURTH DIMENSION PUBLISHING CO., LTD
16 Fifth Avenue, City Layout. PMB. 01164,
Enugu, Nigeria.
Tel+234-42-459969. Fax+234-42-456904.
email: fdpbooks@aol.com, fdpbooks@yahoo.com
Web site: http://www.fdpbooks.com.

Reprinted 1978, 2002

ISBN 978-156-012-6

CONDITIONS OF SALE

Photoset and printed in Nigeria by
Fourth Dimension Publishers, Enugu.

CONTENTS

DEDICATION

FOR:
Madam Fathia Nkrumah
and
Madam Shirley Graham Du Bois
and
Sister Miriam Makeba Carmichael
and
If you don't known why, Reader,
Drop this book and move on;
It wasn't written with you in mind

FOREWORD

Obi Egbuna arrived in Britain on a scholarship from Nigeria. He quickly won success as a novelist, playwright, and political writer. Just as quickly, he grew frustrated and incensed upon seeing how black people were being treated, not only in Britain, but over much of the world, compelling the young writer to pause and ask himself the question: To whom does my talent belong? As Egbuna himself was to tell Bernth Lindfors of the University of Texas in an interview 15 years later, this uncharacteristic and unsubmissive departure from the traditional approach to African literature did not endear this "cheeky" new-generation author to the publishing elite in the western world and, as might be expected, it soon earned him the reputation among critics as the bad boy of Nigerian literature. But he was hardly new to the world of literary criticism himself.

He made an early impact as a literary critic when, for a time, he reviewed books for the London *Sunday Times* under Michael Radcliff.

He made his first mark on the international stage when his dramatised version of his own first novel was chosen to represent Britain in the First World Negro Arts Festival in Dakar, Senegal, in, leading to invitations and visits to the United States and other places. The play itself enjoyed the added distinction in Britain of being the only African drama ever shown on the BBC Television, first on Channel 2, and repeated in the series "Seven Selected Plays" on Channel 1.

He gained home recognition as a "committed" aware writer when he was invited to Konakry by the late Dr. Kwame Nkrumah, then in exile in Guinea and given Nkrumah's now famous "Message to the Black Peoples of Britain," to bring back to England. Upon his return to London, however, he was arrested by the British police for "uttering a threat in writing," and was incarcerated in

Brixton Prison for nearly six months. The result was his internationally explosive and controversial book, *Destroy This Temple*, which he wrote behind bars and launched both in Britain (MacGibbon & Kee Publishers, London) and the United States (William Morrow & Company, Inc., New York). But this bravura resilience did not earn for young Egbuna the freedom from molestation to let him write in peace as his friends had hoped. Perhaps this was inevitable in the racially tense atmosphere of Britain, and perhaps equally inescapable for a creative "rebel" who had overnight become the rallying point of most underdog anti-unfreedom forces seeking intellectual respectability. The harassments against him continued, sometimes hovering on unsubtle attempts at character assassination. Though this continued until he left England, Egbuna's talent for creativity was never in question, his professional dedication far from discouraged. He continued working with top British artists until the end of his stage including Dame Peggy Ashcroft who was featured in the BBC production of his work *Emperor of the Sea*, literally a few days before he left the United Kingdom for good.

But he was to learn upon reaching home, as he shows in this "Diary," that a Nigerian, in defence of his class interest, could be more deadly to a fellow Nigerian than an invading lynch-mob from "Babylon." Having suffered both invasions, he does not mince words which aggrieves him more. His experiences since his return to Enugu have included being the Director of Programmes for the State Television, combining it with the Directorship of the State Writers Workshop, and also writing a weekly column, Author's Diary, in the State newspaper where bits of his "Diary" first appeared in sketches, with enough public enthusiasm and curtain calls to inspire this publication. Meanwhile, the author has, in spite of these other commitments since his return, produced two other books – his latest novel, *The Minister's Daughter*, and his second volume of short stories, *Emperor of the Sea*.

The "essays" which comprise this present volume are

viii

a distillation of the author's ideas and impressions during his many years in exile and since his return. Part 1 deals with his HomeComing to his native Africa after 15 years abroad, while Part 2 is a mirror into the past seen in retrospection. Each "essay" is complete in itself, but taken together, the pieces tell a continuous story narrated in a sort of prose-poetry style.

W. Somerset Maugham once wrote that authors are to be divided into two classes: those for whom literature is a means, and those for whom literature is an end. On reading Obi Egbuna's "Diary" to completion, one begins to wonder if the author has not succeeded in combining the best of both worlds. The joy one gets from the style of the work is enough to lull the reader into the conclusion that here is a writer whose undistracted objective is to give literary gratification. Yet the message of the collection stands out like a mountain peak. For an accomplished exile abroad, to return home is to become powerless, and to remain abroad is to become irrelevant.

There is no exile from exile like an exile in exile in his own home. But, for me, it is the very last "essay", Letter To A Sister (recalled from the author's prison diary), that is the main gem of the book. Alone, it is a book.

Reinhard W. Sander

PART ONE

HOME-COMING

FIRST SIP FROM THE SPRING
OF THE MOUNTAIN

A little white girl once asked me why I do not write poetry. I told her that the wind does not write poetry, because the wind is poetry. Her reaction was an intrigued smile which I was expected to interpret as a homage to my wit. I told her to spare her pretty little white face (and it was pretty) because I was being neither witty nor facetious. I told her that I am a poetic reality because I hail from the land where man has learnt to blend with his landscape. I told her that my voice is the murmur of the sea, my laughter the cackle of the wind, my anger the roar of the lion, and my walk the rhythm of the palm tree dancing in the wind. I told her that for me to write poetry is to dismantle my being, to say that I am beautiful, to masturbate myself. I told her that what will feed my people is not masturbation, but revolution. I told her that I am no longer interested in the greenness of the Iroko tree, but only in how many guns I can carve out of its bulkness.

But today, as I come back to my homeland after an absence of 15 years, as I stand here on this soil of the palm trees, surveying the landscape of my birth, as I feel the pulse of Africa beating once more like tom-tom in my veins, I feel the need to cry out: let's (oh do LET'S) masturbate a little. Just for now. The roar of honking sports cars has been replaced by the purr of the wind. The barking of police dogs has given way to the singing of birds. Sex under the imprisonment of bedsheets is now a thing of the past (if you've never had a black woman under a tropical palm-tree, boy! you are still a virgin). You lie on the grass when it is all over, no blankets to pick off the floor. As I stand here in the womb of nature, loving nature, feeling nature, seeing people, little people, big people, fat people, thin people, beautiful people, ugly people (for where there is poverty, there is also

3

ugliness), and marvelling at the defiant beauty of the dehu-
manized daughters of our soil, familiar words from "Women
and Socialism" echo loud and clear in my ears: "Let no one
underrate his own power, or imagine that one more or less
makes no difference. No one, not even the weakest can be
dispensed with for furthering the progress, and the rights of
humanity. A continual dropping hollows out the hardest
stone. And many drops make the brook, and brooks make
the stream, and streams the great river, whose majestic
course can be stopped by no obstacle in nature. Precisely
the same thing applies to the cultural life of humanity.
Nature is everywhere our instructress, and if we abide by
her teaching, the final victory must be ours."

To live here is to know the poor people of this earth, the
real people of this earth, to cancel winter, to drink palm-
wine from the calabash that also grows from this earth, to
learn the wisdom of our soil, to know that I cannot hide
from the Truth because the Truth resides in my blood, to sip
eternally from the spring of the mountain, flowing eternally,
growing eternally, singing eternally – oh yes, to admit that
the springs of the mountain will forever please me more the
sea – Guantanamera!

MEETING MOTHER
(after fifteen years)

To call her a bag of bones would be a cruel understatement. For how can you call a tooth-pick a bag! Where there was once flesh is now dry bone. What was once the voice of a bell now rasps like a battered gong. Laughter that once caressed like the kiss of the wind is now a yarn with the hiss of a sigh. Eyes that once sparkled with joy and merriment now flicker between myopia and total sight oblivion. She literally rattles as she walks, purrs like a lazy wind as she talks, and actually thanks God at the end of each day for this "happy life" of hers.

This is the figure which haunted me these past many years in England. Whatever I did or tried to do, I kept seeing in my mind's eye the figure of this scraggy suffering widow, this Mother of mine, walking bare-footed, and sore-footed, and all sweaty, all the way from my home town of Ozubulu to my boarding school at Nnewi, to bring me a couple of coconuts, wrapped in ragged handkerchiefs, while "luckier" mothers and fathers arrived in luxury cars to bring my classmates unbelievable pocket money. Mother suffered and sacrificed everything for me, her one and only son, and I promised never to let her down, like the one and only Sun in the jaded horizon of our life. To bring (even if only) a flicker of a smile to that face of hers, I did everything within the power of a fatherless teenage pauper. And I knew that the only way a poor nobody's son like me could make it in life was by beating the sons of those richer parents both in exam-rooms, and on athletic tracks. And I even dreamt youthful dreams of making school history by becoming the first Senior Prefect to pass out in Grade One. Life became for me an endless soul-grinding decathlon, like climbing a rocky hill bare-footed, dawn after dawn, in the biting chillness of harmattan cruel wind, just to fetch water

5

from a fountain of sustenance, which drip-dripped in tiny trickles, out of hidden crevices in the rocky realities of life. It seemed endless but I made it in the end. But it was only the beginning.

Still pursued by the phantom of that hungry-faced woman, the face of that Mother of mine, I took a scholarship to England where, I believed, lay the answer to her plight. But I did not reckon with the choice I had to make. That choice was between accepting a bribe of academic worthiness to return to Africa to feed Mother through creating other hungrier mothers than her, or to reject the bribe, pick up the pen or the armour, or probably both in that order, even if it meant more suffering and pain for Mother and me, till real salvation is won for all. Unselfish as I knew Mother was, I was convinced which choice she would want me to make. And I made it! Bringing back home to Mother and Africa academic laurels, granted by the very potentates who have anguished millions of black mothers like mine through economic ambush is a measure of self-deception unworthy of the son of a mother like mine! I took the other road, which I am still plodding today.

As I look at you now, Mother, this first day of my return from England to Africa, seeing you as you are this very minute, 15 years older, 15 years thinner, 15 years weaker, 15 years poorer, and myself 15 years still less able to help you, I do not regret making that choice (Time only dilutes the convictions of the weak). If anything, it has emboldened my resolve. I will die an uncompromising fighter against the oppressors of the poor, a dedicated servant of Truth and Peace, a dialectical materialist and an eternal hater of evil and sham, because I'm motivated by that unquenchable love for goodness which I want for our major humanity who, like Mother, have been drinking waters of affliction all their lives under the boots of international Mac-the-knives.

Please, whoever you are reading these lines of mine, I

want you to now say hello to Mother, my long-suffering black mother, my eternal source of literary and revolutionary inspiration, the scraggy figure in whose womb lay the robust Africa of tomorrow!

MEETING MY PEOPLE

It was like the bursting of a dam. They came like an armada of cyclones. They ran from their farms. They leapt down from the palm trees. They surged from the bottom of the valley. They stampeded from the top of the hills. And from what seemed a wilderness of mud huts a moment ago, they crawled out in hundreds like lizards from the crevices of a rock. These were my people. Loin-cloth men from the land of the palm trees. They howled like wild winds from the bowels of the forest. And they vied with each other to shake my hands, to queue for the contents of my near-empty wallet, to embrace me, to carry me shoulder-high, to crown me a village hero because, to them, to come back from the land of the white men is the nearest a man can get to being a white man, to being a God!

It was then that it hit met between the eyes like a bullet. The worst calamity that can ever befall a writer is to write for an audience that cannot read. My books suddenly devalued to mere blades of grass between hard covers. But even this is a generous assessment, for a blade of grass is at least a thing of beauty, a source of greenness, of food, of medicine, of life, but what is the page of a book to a man who cannot read? A rectangle of whiteness crawling with bizarre micro reptiles, characters perpetually mocking the peasant of his ignorance, of his helplessness, of his inferiority, of his shame! How can I tell these people falling at my feet how they fill me with disgust? How can I tell them that I loathe them to extinction because I love them to extinction? How can I tell them to crawl back into their graves because "a hard rain is gonna fall?" How can I tell them they're worshipping at the wrong shrine because this god does not believe in worshipping, only in justice? How can I tell them that my god is the god thunder and lightning, of fire and whipcord! How can I explain to them that the solution to

8

their problem is in themselves, not in the land of the white man? How can I tell them it is they Africa needs, not black white-men? How can I tell them Africa is asleep today because they themselves are asleep today, that Africa will recover her strength the day they themselves discover their strength, that power lies in the countryside, not in slave-markets called cities. How can I explain Che's meaning that ten city intellectuals are worth less than one farmer from the village, that the African problem can never be solved by the African "Elite" because the African "Elite" is part of the problem? How can I tell them I have nothing to offer them but what they already have, but fail to recognise? How can I explain to them that, like Paul Robeson, it is in England I have discovered Africa? How can I tell them that no son of Africa who goes to England and does not discover Africa is a fraud? How can I tell them that my England was no Alladin's cave of palaces and queens, of Nelson's Column and Trafalgar Square, of Westminster and 10 Downing Street, that my England was the ghettoes of Brixton and Notting Hill Gate, Perry Bar and Birmingham, of smelly Croydon and Alexandra Road? How can I tell them I have brought home no academic triumphs and vouchers to rob, only pain, death and resurrection? How can I tell them I have brought home neither foreign aid nor kilograms of Oxfam meat, only a programme for the abolition of the necessity for both? How can I explain my record of imprisonment, the scars on my body, the organised mutilation of my character? How does a man explain that his body is scarred only because his mind is pure, that his head is carved up only because his sanity is intact, that he is ugly only because he is beautiful. How can I tell them I am the first arrival of a new breed, the first drop of the coming storm, the first among a generation of new Blacks who go to England, not to seek "life," but only to die in order to live?

THE LAST VISITOR

The parcel was delivered by a nun. I can remember it well. How can I forget the young smile on her old face? Watching her get off her bicycle that beautiful dawn was like watching a bird – a black head, white plumage – alight on a field in the rising sun. A serene sight to the eye, almost an apparition in a village where suffering has made such happy faces rare.

The church bells were sobbing in the distance, as if in writhing pain for the agony of the poor. The wind, even more desperately, was howling like a hungry wolf in the forests. And when the bicycle bell tinkled the arrival of the lady visitor, the chickens started cakling as if in fright.

The nun propped her bicycle against the wall and then asked my name. She wanted to make sure I was the "man" she had come to see. Obviously she had expected an older person, in a more imposing surrounding. And the fact that I was bare-footed, and casually seated on the bare floor outside our house, didn't help. It wasn't really much of a house. I confess it is a little misleading to call it a house at all. Truth told, it was only a tiny hut, with walls of mud, a ceiling of bamboo poles, all capped on top with palm-thatch, giving the roof the shape of a match-box that had been sliced diagonally in half.

I was always a shy person by nature. But when the nun smiled, I forgot my shyness and warmed up to her. But in spite of her outward loveliness of composure and geniality, I could guess that the lady was greatly disturbed inside, and that her call was not a casual visit.

She confirmed this at once, by telling me that her business was urgent. And she came straight to the point. She was in fact a Reverend Sister attached to the Joint Hospital not far from my home. A man was dying at this hospital, she said. Everything medically possible had already been done

10

for this man. But it was no use. He had less than two hours to live. "But why come to tell me all this?" I asked. What had all this to do with me? Then the nun explained. She said that the dying old man had made one last with. His very last request. It was a strange request, to say the least, but a dying man's wish must be respected, she said. The dying old man wanted someone to come to his bedside and read him a poem. If not a poem, any beautiful literary passage from a book to lull him to his last and eternal sleep. In answer to my questions, the nun admitted to me quite candidly that the dying man did not ask for me specifically. He did not even know that I existed. The reason that they had come to me was that I was the only one for miles around who qualified to do this reading, according to the man's primary condition. Even more puzzled than before, I prayed the nun to tell me what this necessary condition was, and why they had decided that I was the only one who qualified for miles around. Then she replied that the man had requested that the reader must be a "Non-Believer." It appears that the man had done a lot of travelling in his life, and had known countless disappointments. Everything upon which he had pinned his faith had let him down. Finally he had come to the conclusion that nothing was worth believing. And now, as he was breathing his last on his death bed, he wanted a fellow non-believer to read something to lull him to a happy death. That was why they had decided that I qualified. I was a "non-believer," she said in conclusion.

I listened to the nun's story patiently. When she finished, I told her politely that she had come to the wrong man. I did not qualify to do this reading. Far from being a non-believer, I was in fact a strong believer. I believe in Truth. I believe in People. I worship daily on the holy alter of Beauty. I believe in Love. I believe in Me. I am, therefore I am. I believe in Life. I believe in Freedom. I believe in the Equality of all men. I believe in the universal Brotherhood of Man. I believe in the Ultimate Triumph of Justice. I believe in Tomorrow's Sunrise. At this point, the nun

11

placed her forefinger across my lips and said sh-sh-sh! And with a saintly smile on her face, she asked me if I also believed in granting the last wishes of dying men. She had won.

Two minutes later, we were on our way to the hospital. But the tragedy was that we were late. The man had died before we got there. The corpse was on the bed, wearing an expression of relief, the expression of a man who had escaped it all.

As I looked through the window of the ward, I saw a little flower dancing in the wind. And sitting on a tiny branch of that flower, there was a tiny black bird with a spanning long tail. Both flower and bird were looking pitilessly divine. The bird was singing a sad song. I started wondering if the bird had composed that song specially for the dead old man. And it began to click. The more I listened to that birdsong, the more I realised its significance. It was not really a song. It was a poem. I asked a young nurse how long that bird had been reciting that poem out there in the garden. The nurse said it was at least an hour. The bird had been singing out there for at least half hour before the old man died. Yes, the old man had had his last wish granted after all. By that bird in the garden. The mystery bird had read him his last poem as he had requested. I wasn't sure whether or not the bird qualified as a "Non-Believer," but from the expression on the dead man's face, it was clear that he had enjoyed the sounds that had greeted his ears in his dying moments.

The wind laughed in the faraway hills. And the sky was a fascinating grotesquerie of colours. Almost surrealistic. Breathtaking. Suddenly, I felt a hand touch me on the shoulder. I turned. It was the nun. She said she would like to know, out of sheer curiosity, what poem I would have read the dying old man, if we had met him in time. I confessed to her that I had found it a difficult choice to make. How could one satisfy a man whose belief was non-belief? But finally, I had settled for a passage from Oscar Wilde's DE PRO-FUNDIS. And this was what it would have sounded like:

"I have hills far steeper to climb, valleys much darker to

12

pass through. And I have to get it all out of myself. Neither religion, morality, nor reason can help me at all. Morality does not help me. I am a born antinomian. I am one of those who are made for exceptions, not for laws. But while I see that there is nothing wrong in what one does, I see that there is something wrong in what one becomes. It is well to have learned that.

"Religion does not help me. The faith that others give to what is unseen, I give to what one can touch, and look at. My gods dwell in temples made with hands, and within the circle of actual experience is my creed made perfect and complete: too complete, it may be, for like many or all of those who have placed their heaven in this earth, I have found in it not merely the beauty of heaven, but the horror of hell also. When I think about religion at all, I feel as if I would like to found an order for those who cannot believe: the Confraternity of the Faithless, one might call it, where on an alter, on which no taper burned, a priest, in whose heart peace had no dwelling, might celebrate with unblessed bread and a chalice empty of wine. Everything to be true must become a religion. And agnosticism should have its ritual no less than faith. It has sown its martyrs, it should reap its saints, and praise God daily for having hidden Himself from man. But whether it be faith or agnosticism, it must be nothing external to me. Its symbols must be of my own creating. Only that is spiritual which makes its own form. If I may not find its secret within myself, I shall never find it; if I have not got it already, it will never come to me."

"Reason does not help me. It tells me that the laws under which I am convicted are wrong and unjust laws, and the system under which I have suffered a wrong and unjust system. But, somehow, I have got to make both of these things just and right to me. And exactly as in Art one is only concerned with what a particular thing is at a particular moment to oneself, so it is also in the ethical evolution of one's character. I have got to make everything that has happened to me good for me."

13

MEETING AN OLD GIRLFRIEND

She ran out of her room, took one look at me, and screamed. Hardly what I expected from an old girlfriend whom I was seeing for the first time after my many years in England.

"But you look awful", she cried. "You are not what I expected you to look like, you're not dressed like a "Been-to," you're not handsome anymore, you're not robust, you're not fresh, you don't even wear a suit with striped trousers, like lawyers and other men just returned from England."

Which reminds me, I replied quietly, you mustn't come too close either. For I am a T.B.-suspect as well. Though I was teasing, my heart was smouldering under my ribs, and the smoke was bitter. Can it really be, I asked myself, that our society has descended to this level of cultural rot and confusion that a man is no longer considered well-dressed till he has a loin-cloth knotted around his neck and calls it a Tie? And the irony of it all is, that if that same man, were to remove that loin-cloth from his neck, and would do the proper thing by tying it where it properly belongs, around his loins, gracing the equator of the human body, garbing in mysterious concealment the headquarters of his holy of holies, the dignity and clean beauty of his manhood, they will call him a savage.

I looked at my Black Sister where she stood, my ex-girl friend, her beauty was there, her strength was there, and my head echoed words I had read in a book somewhere; this beautiful black tigress radiated the strength of a silken veil, black, transparently thin, but closely woven with threads of fine fibre, dark and soft as an Indian sari. Her voice was still as I remembered it while in England, like a bird-song coming across a large expense of a nameless lake on a rain-less night. Beautiful, yes. But something has gone wrong. Perilously wrong. Painfully wrong. Tragically woeful.

14

I read somewhere in a book that rocking a child to sleep is almost similar to the effect of opium. It harms him physically and mentally and affects his moral growth, because it has an impact on the brain, and, consequently, on the entire organism. Cradle-rocking, they say, arose in olden times, not for the benefit of the child, but for the convenience of the parents. In order not to waste time, the mother spun while rocking the cradle with her foot.

As I stood there, watching this woman that had for so long been rocked to sleep by outsiders to the point of no longer recognising her Brother, I wanted to say so much to her, but my lips were unable to find words to express the grim magnitude of feelings welling up inside me like a long shadow of nagging despair. I had by profession studied the art of reading faces, and could see through her mask and shampooed hair that she was only shamming happiness and sophistication, the expression on her face reminded me of a cowering dog threatened with stick. She was like a broken blade of grass that had been mercilessly trampled in the dust. That dust was there evident on her face, but she had been taught to call it powder. Saturday Night Powder, when the plain fact was that the midnight in her soul was in danger of becoming perennial. It was not her hair that needed shampooing, it was her mind, and I wanted to cry when I recollected what a wonderful soul was being crushed out of shape in that lovely body that used to be my lone-moment solace, my angel in ebony, years ago in childhood days gone. This was what men had done to my black candle, a candle that used to warm the alter of my libido with her red flame. They had "educated" her, not explained her, they had put her on a history train without telling her her destination, and she had become unconscious of who she was, where she was going, even what time of day it was. She had forgotten it was dawn, time to wake up, to shake off the hangover of being rocked to sleep by parents that weren't even hers. I saw in my one-time love, a one-time spiritual millionairess who had become bankrupt through investing too heavily in the materialism of life. I saw this bankruptcy mirrored in her eyes, the self hatred that was so

15

deeply embedded she didn't even realise it was there. I wanted to hear her scream in continuous auto-suggestion, till she was cured, the words: "My skin is black, my nose is broad, my lips are thick, and I AM BEAUTIFUL." I wanted to fall down on my knees and beg her to get off the corridor of the doomed. For then and only then would she begin to see me as I AM, instead of (judging me with transplanted eyes) as I look. I admit I look battered, thin, ugly, penniless, scarred, barefooted, and battleworne, but one cannot expect to fight for the lives of other men 24 hours a day without being bruised and depolished a little. I wanted to think aloud as Felix Dzerzhinsky once thought aloud under a similar historical confrontation in Warsaw Citadel. I wanted to make my ex-girl gone astray keep quiet for a moment and hear me present my case in these few words:

In reality, he who lives as I do, cannot live very long. I can neither hate nor love by halves. I simply cannot give only half my spirit. I either give all or nothing. I have drunk from the cup of life not only all the bitterness, but also all the sweetness, and if somebody should say to me: look at the furrows on your brow, at your emaciated body, at your present life, look and you will see that life has broken you, I should reply in these words: no, life has not broken me, it is I who have broken life; it is not life that has taken everything from me, it is I who have taken everything, literally everything, all I want, namely myself, from it. Yes, people have created riches for themselves, and these riches, these inanimate things, have fettered their creators so that people live for riches, not riches for people. So don't be cross for my convictions, my dear lovely Black angel, there is no place in them for hatred of people. You misunderstand me if you think there is. I have hated wealth because I have loved people; I have hated oppressors because I am only a splinter from a soil scotched with colonial oppression, because I see and feel with all my heart that today people worship the golden calf which has turned the human spirit into something animal-like, chasing all love from the heart.

16

Remember that in the soul of such as myself there is a sacred flame which gives happiness even at stake.

Yes, I wanted to say all this, to pour out my soul to my ex-girl who seemed to have forgotten that my purpose of going to England, as I promised before departure, was to make myself intelligent, not intellectual. I wanted to say this to her, and more. But no. I couldn't. All I succeeded in doing was shake my head in wounded surrender, mumbled a few words of good-bye, and leave. The expression on my face said the rest.

To my surprise, she seemed to have understood. Never underrate the power of our women, they can read the soul of their men, beautiful dears, like a razor eating into the core of afufa. The girl gave me a long thoughtful look. She had guessed at once that those few muffled words of clumsy goodbye was my clumsy way of asking her to make a choice before I reached her front gate. To choose my way? Or the way of the neo-Toms? To choose between my style and the style of other (Black-is-shameful) Been-toes? To choose me and Africa, or them and Europe? Either, or. I saw her face contort as she pondered these questions in her mind.

Then suddenly she smiled, ran forward, and engulfed me in an embrace which brought back many beautiful memories. And still holding me tight in the groove and warmth of her Kosoerect bosom, she explained merrily:

"At least, I have nothing to fear from you but T.B."

It was the nicest compliment ever paid to a T.B. suspect.

17

THE SUSPENSE

This is absolutely a true story. It happened only yesterday. I was travelling to Lagos from Enugu by air. Suddenly, the woman sitting next to me had a strange attack and collapsed. She was pregnant. She died before the plane touched down, but not before she had thrust a piece of paper in my hands. It was an incomplete letter which, even till this moment, makes neither head nor tail to me. This is the content of that letter.

"My darling child,

If the solicitors carry out my instructions, you will not see this letter till you are twenty-one. And if my doctor's prediction is correct, I will not be around till then. This is probably the first time in human history that a woman ever wrote a letter to a baby still in her womb. You must remember this. At the time I am writing, you are no more than a nameless anticipation kicking within me. Only the angels in heaven know whether you are going to be a boy or a girl. But it doesn't matter. I want you to concentrate hard on this true story of my life. I say this because, by the time you are twenty-one, you shall have heard countless versions of it. History shall have bandied it from generation to generation, facts shall have metamorphosed into propaganda, propaganda into legend. This terrifies me. I have lived to see history which is supposed to be an analysis of the past to explain the present turn into a distortion of the present to justify the past. I would hate to see this fate befall the realities of my present concern. The reason for this will soon be obvious to you, my darling child.

I arrived in Africa seven years ago. I was no longer a little girl. At nearly thirty, I had grown into a woman who had ceased to see life as one harmless huge bed of roses, having been pricked too many times to be completely blind to its countless thorns. This is the fate of every Black woman born

18

in America today. I had nothing when I arrived in Nigeria and, in many ways I suppose, was nothing. I was unmarried, lonely and unknown. I had signed a three-year contract with the government of this country to teach in a girl's school in a little village which I will not name here. To some people in America, this might have been a mere adventure, an escape, a hibernation from a life of turmoil in New York. But they would tell you that they are coming to bring civilisation to the cultural barren land of Africa. Stuffed with preconceived notions of Africa, they would expect to be crushed by the sheer weight of poverty surrounding people of the Niger, to stifle in the spiritual vacuum of a black pagan country, to swoon in the stench of abject slovenliness which, to them, is Africa. But to me, dear child, it was different. In fact, it was the other way round. I presumed nothing. Instead, I found myself, at nearly thirty years of age, asking myself all over again, the really true meanings to such simple things as "Poverty," and "Culture," and the whole purpose of life. Who frankly is a poor man? A man looking resplendent in a thousand-dollar silk suit to whom life is one constant oscillation between sex-change surgery and the psychiatric couch? Or is it a man who may be covered in rags but whose soul shines with the nobility of man? Is a poor man really a person who has little? Or is it in fact a man who wants much? Africa confronted me with these questions, especially after the way I had known America. And the more I delved into their answers, the more staggered I was at my new findings. I began to realise how different the reputation of a people could be from their real valuation. Africa became like the surface of a mirror: the longer I concentrated on it, the more I saw of my own image. I began to feel a new transition going on within me. When I was younger, I had imagined that, to understand a country, all one had to do was to appreciate how its people blended with its topography. Africa proved me wrong. There is much more to it. I came to learn that every judgement you pass on a people is a judgement on your own self. A judgement on your own criterion of judgement. How

19

great or how small you find a people depends almost entirely on your own power of observation, your basis of evaluation, and to what extent you consider your own doxy as the only one orthodoxy. It boils down to this. The recorded measurement of any object, far from being the absolute measure of that object, is in fact the measure of the measuring capability of the measurer. This is the first lesson Africa teaches (or should teach) an intelligent visitor from the West. I had flown thousands of miles from America to learn this lesson. And I am grateful. But the final scales did not actually begin to fall from my eyes till the one day I will never forget till I die, the day I witnessed the realisation of the dream of a lifetime, the day I met the one man I knew I was born to marry. Yes, my darling child, the happiest day of my life was the day I met your father. All through my life, it was my ambition to one day marry an African, a man from the very soil from where my grandparents were once taken away to America as slaves. And though I knew in my heart of hearts that this my cherished dream could come true one day, I had no idea that I would be so lucky to meet a Nigerian man as gloriously beautiful and sublime as your father. Unfortunately, his people did not accept me. Because to them, though my skin was even blacker than theirs, I was still a "white" woman. And to make matters worse, my doctor told me, soon after my marriage, that I could not have a child and live. I could of course be pregnant and have a child, said the doctor, but I was bound to die during the actual delivery of the child. Even an operation could not save me, the doctor said with finality. I kept this secret from my husband. You see, I had made up my mind what to do. I knew that, as long as I was alive, I would always be a huge cause of conflict between my husband and his family. And the very last thing I wanted to do was to come between the man I love and the people who love him enough to consider me unequal for his love. On the other hand, I knew that if I become pregnant and bear him a child, though some people might see my baby as a fulfilment of an omen, judging from the nature of my death in the childbirth, I shall be a happy

20

woman in the gladness of knowing that I have left my husband something to remember me by. I will wish him to marry again, and forget me as quickly as he can. I will want his family to know that, even in my hour of death, I love them to adoration, because, for me, it is not possible to love an apple fruit and hate the apple tree. As for you, my darling child, I want you to love and respect your new mother, as if she was your real mother. I don't want you ever to feel like a motherless orphan, because death has not come to me as a surprise. Tell people with pride that your mother died in order to give you flesh, just as the word was made flesh in the Bible. Some people might consider me the American female Othello, a woman who loved not too wisely but too well. But I don't care. They say it is better to have loved and lost, than not to have loved at all. If I must be remembered at all, I want to be remembered, not as a person, but as an aspect of a history that is Black America today, a history which will compel an analysis of the past to guide the present, and not as an apology for the past to avoid the solutions of the present. So my darling child, as I say goodbye, I leave this envelope of love for you to . . . ."

Dear Reader, this is exactly how the letter ended in mid-sentence. This is as far as the pregnant Black American woman got before she collapsed and died on our plane to Lagos. Okay, okay, I admit. It was not really a true story. I made it up while flying to Lagos on Tuesday, the 27th of May, this year. I was sitting next to the window on the plane. The pilot, Captain Osakwe, was doing his thing up front. Two beautiful air-stewardesses were looking after us passengers with commendable effusiveness and charm. Suddenly I got into a poetic mood. Africa sprawled before me down below like a tamed lion. I likened the hump of the distant landscape to the croupe of a crouching lion, a lone palm tree standing on the slopy end depicting the tail of this imaginary lion, the promontory adjoining the opposite end being the head, with manes of wild green vegetation, and an eye of blazing roundness, the rising sun. I was so carried away by this literary flight of imagination that, before I

21

knew what I was doing. I had taken out my pen and, inspired by a pregnant woman sitting in front of me, I was actually writing a story in the form of the above letter. But I could not complete it before our plane landed in Lagos. And after catching a rickety old taxi, and going through the hellish experience of Lagos bumpy roads and choking traffic jams to my hotel, the inspiration had left me altogether. So I decided to leave the story as it was, and just keep it a suspense. I hope I haven't ruined it too much for you, dear Reader. Better luck next time.

MEETING ROSEMARIE —
THE VIRGIN PROSTITUTE

To know is to be miserable. To suffer. To know that you do not know. But to know enough to realise how cruel man is to his fellow man. To be toothless through gnashing. To be lonely. Sad. A voice in the wilderness. I know. I feel it now. Lying beside me on this hotel bed, as I write, is a black girl (Rosemarie) who has been my welcome-home Jamila these past two nights. She is a prostitute. A good one. (shocked? — pitiful hypocrite! — or plain jealous?) Yes, she is "fantabulous." She knows her job. Oh yes, she knows her job (I can vouch for that!) She knows the trade front and backwards. But little else. Very little else in fact. I envy her. God! how I envy her. She is so deliciously innocent. Some people would say ignorant. But she knows peace on a level I can never attain in a hundred years. For her, there is no capitalism, no Guavara/Debray foco theory, no Nkrumah, no Malcolm X, no Fanon or Carlos Marighela, no anti-Freud androgynous youth culture, no Pablo-ing of Picasso or Neruda, nor pebbling of Surrealistic ceramics, no dialectical materialism, no pain. God is responsible for everything. That's all. (She told me endless stories how men had cheated her, black men, white men, in this very Enugu posh hotel, but to her it is all God's will). She is so sadly vulnerable, so delectably blank, so pure, so clean, so unspoilt, so untainted, so unpenetrated, so unpenetrating, so virgin in mind! Jesus! By her own admission, she does not even know how to "eat" her breakfast. And taking a bath in my hotel room, Western-style, is a special treat for her. And she comes out dripping wet because she is afraid to use the hotel towel. In a few minutes' time, I'll be bidding her good-bye forever, and she'll be walking away brimming with laughter and blissful abandon, while I'll continue writhing in the agony of knowing that I do not know, that both of us,

23

Rosemarie and I, as we go our separate ways, are two black pigmies in mobile prison-cells. And THE TRAGEDY is she envies me! God! Why does one have to reach a level of knowing where one fears to know? Why? On why ...

Where are you now, my dark-eyed Oyoko? As you take your holy communion this Sunday morn, can you spare a thought for the "mysterious" Brother who took you for his first communion with his native felt for many a year? Where have you flown now, my dark-eyed Afrobird? I remember the sun pouring through the hotel windows, with heated jealousy, as my head lay peacefully on your lap. I remember watching your face intently, your eyes were half-closed, the lashes formed two shadows right under your eyes, two dark shadows shaped and arched like two broken wings of a bird. I remember you starting to sing a song which reminded me of my mother in her younger days. I have been to many faraway lands in my time, lands where begging children, carrying corpses of their younger brothers and sisters, sang laments of parents who also died of hunger; but never before in my life had I been so moved by a song. Yours shattered my defences that sweet sad dawn. Your voice flickered inside me like a living flame, lighting up the memory lane of my childhood years till I could see in my mind's eye my father's grave in St. Kevin's churchyard, the little hibiscus flower I had planted afterwards outside our house, my telling Mama not to worry because God would provide, only to find out soon enough that God didn't pay school fees. I remember rising from the bed, and you following me into the bathroom. I remember how you leaned over the washbasin, how you scooped the water with your hand, how you splashed it on your breasts, and how the water snaked down you lustily like the Serpent on the body of Eve. I remember your natural Afro beauty, your low-swung breasts, your thighs, sinuous, long, wild, dark, titilating, magic to the touch. I remember your skill, executed with power-conscious pliability of the steel blade. I remember all the maidens of this land, of Enugu's New Haven, of Obiagu

Road, of Uwani, of Ihiala, of Port Harcourt, of Owerri, of Yola, of Kaduna, of Surulere, of Nigeria, of Kenya, of Tanzania, all the women of Africa who, like you, have been babied, doodled, and sullied to death unsung.

Where are you now, my dark-eyed Sister? You were like an apple that fell off a tree before it had time to ripen. A little apple spoilt and aborted by worms, you were like a baby bird exhausted from many unsuccessful attempts at first solo flight, a broken little orphan-bird I had found and taken home for a temporary emotional refuelling we both needed. You were like a token grave of a stillborn babe, and all I did was add to the weird irony by planting there the crooked cross of a crooked bliss. Yes, I now give the selfrighteous human-gods this opportunity to laugh at my "weak" fall for a "prostitute," but dear Sister, is an admission of "weakness" not in itself a manifestation of strength, and would you not prefer (for a brother) an honest weakling to a strong hypocrite?

How long will you remain the voiceless echo from a long-dead present, the perennial symbol of the foreign defloration of our maidenhood, a broken blade of grass to be trampled upon, guideless in both sorrow and joy? How long, I ask, how long? How long will it take you to hear my cry, my lovely Sister, how much longer will you ignore my call? Are you truly awaiting the dawn of my execution so that you can proclaim me a martyr, proceed to walk on my hide with pride, and then argue, in logic foreign to our native ways, that the leopard-skin has no value till the leopard is dead and skinned?

Oh yes, women of this land, of this continent, you who have been debauched, and defaced and depersonalized, when will you rise to fight your defilement? Oh ye Rosie-souled prostitutes of Blackville, when will one of you, just one, get up that Kilimanjero peak and, like Aitmatov's beautiful Altynai, raise the clarion call: Rise from your graves, you poor women! Ghosts of all those raped, sullied women, deprived of human dignity, rise! Rise, martyrs and make the old, hideously wicked world quake! It is I who am calling you, I, the last of you, I who have suffered this fate and defied it!

When is it someone, somewhere, someday, will, in the style of Australia's Dorothy Hewitt, make the air over this continent resound to the cry:

And all the roads of Africa,
Are thick with marching Girls;
For every girl mauled to death,
A girl will rise again.

BED TIME STORY

A friend's little boy said to me one night:

"You tell us nice bed-time stories whenever you come visiting, Uncle Obi. I like them when they're good, because they make us laugh. And I like them even better when they're not so good, because they lull us nicely to sleep, and we children can play guessing games the next day, trying to guess how the story must have ended after we had fallen asleep. I like to be proud that I have an uncle who, as you once put it, is a story-farmer by profession. I like to think that you are a kind man, because you take us for walks to the hilltops, and talk to us about the beauty of nature, the sweet hum of the birds, and how sad it is that man is the only animal that kills for laughs. I like to tell them at school that you take us for rides in that little cuddly green car of yours which they call the Mini-muck; but you tell us it is only an engine wearing a danshiki, a peasant on wheels, that it is the humblest, yet the healthiest of cars, because having a ride in it is like having an air-shower in the sun, to know the sweetness of motion, and to feel nature's kiss on your face. I like to talk about you to my friends, with pride, with love, without stopping because you are the kindest man we know since our Papa died. But the rich kids at school say that their parents and their friends in England call you a thorn in the flesh. They say the English tried to kill you in Britain, and even put you in jail. And though you've been lucky so far in staying alive after so many scars on your young body and bold spirit, they swear they'll get you some day and clamp a crown of thorns on your head. Tell me, Uncle Obi, why do they hate you so?"

I stood there staring at the young little boy in silence, as if transfixed to the floor. To say that I was flabbergasted and flummoxed would be high-sounding, yet inadequate to express how I felt at that moment. I was literally unable to

27

open my mouth. I, the restless gymnast of the Kung Fu of words, could not find words for once to fight my way through a little boy's innocence of a simple question. And it is not surprising, for how can you explain to a mere child that life is never a bed of roses for any craftsman whose raw material is truth? I did not even know where to start. But just then, by sheer luck of coincidence, my eyes caught a big bible lying on a nearby table. That did the trick. It put an idea into my head, and I told the children what was not really a story, but a reminder of an old one.

I told them the story of the little Jewish boy from Nazareth. He too was hounded by the potentates of his day. Not because he was rich (he had no money). Not because he claimed to be the son of God (they didn't believe him). Not because he was Jewish (his own people hated him most). They crucified him for the same reason they crucified other prophets before him. He told them the truth about themselves. He dared moneylenders to DESTROY THIS TEMPLE, and for that, he had to be crucified between two thieves who were not half as crooked as the men who ordered their crucifixion.

By this time, the children had fallen asleep and, as I watched their beautiful young faces, I could not help wondering what sort of a future awaited these lovely kids in the years of tense international high-noon ahead. My head was so full of speculations and fear that I could not sleep. It occurred to me that my only hope of getting any wink of sleep that night was to find somebody else to tell me a boring bed-time story. So I tip-toed out of the children's room, went downstairs into the library of my host, sat myself comfortably down, and pleaded with Kahlil Gibrain to tell me a bed-time story. He decided on the subject of "Defeat" and this was what he said:

"Defeat, my Defeat, my solitude and my aloofness;
You are dearer to me than a thousand triumphs,
And sweeter to my heart than all world-glory.
Defeat, my Defeat, my self-knowledge and my defiance,

28

Through you I know that I am yet young and swift of foot.
And not to be trapped by withering laurels.
And in you I have found aloneness
And the joy of being shunned and scorned.
Defeat, my Defeat, my shining sword and shield,
In your eyes I have read
That to be enthroned is to be enslaved,
And to be understood is to be levelled down,
And to be grasped is but to reach one's fulness
And like a ripe fruit to fall and be consumed.
Defeat, my Defeat, my bold companion,
You shall hear my songs and my cries and my silences,
And none but you shall speak to me of the beating of wings
And urging of seas,
And of mountains that burn in the night,
And you alone shall climb my steep and rocky soul.
Defeat, my Defeat, my deathless courage,
You and I shall laugh together with the storm,
And together we shall dig graves for all that die in us,
And we shall stand in the sun with a will,
And we shall be dangerous."

29

BLIND DATE

My auntie pleaded with me to meet this Super-girl. My auntie's husband taunted me to no end to meet this Wonder Belle.

Even a Dean of the University hinted insistently I should meet this Psychedelic Sex-magic in motion. Yes, everybody howled that I should meet this heaven-on-earth of a woman! She is glamorous to the point of stardom, they yelled. She is as witty as ten barristers-at-law put together, they lauded. Her academic career reads like something out of the diary of W.E.B. DuBois, they claimed. At 22, she is already a Research Fellow at her Alma-Mata University, and would be knocking off her Ph.D. at the precocious age of 25, they acclaimed. Clearly the ideal woman for a young literary "Been-to" just back from England like yourself (myself, hmm!), they crooned and swooned.

Only one word of warning though! they added, make sure she does not maul you to pieces with her conversation and sophistication!

The die was cast! My meeting her was as inevitable as tomorrow's sunrise.

She had expressed her desire to give me a look-over, and her word, the word of the campus queen, was law! When we did meet, it was like the setting of a drama. We were tricked into a room in the home of my host, my auntie's husband, and were literally locked-up in there, to bask in the cosy sunshine of our compatibility. We were let out two hours later, like two giant panders from the cage of a London zoo, amidst the glare of inquisitive eyes, all bulging with one unspoken question. It was my auntie who first found voice to confront me with it:

"How was she?" she asked, "tell us, don't keep us in suspense, how did you find her?"

How should I know, I replied, I have not even met the woman yet.

30

"What kind of an answer is that?" whispered my auntie, "you were in there two hours with the woman."

I certainly was two hours in there with something in a micro mini-skirt, I admitted, but whatever it was, it clearly was neither woman nor human. She had reminded me of a shudder I had experienced when, earlier that day, I had seen two hunters carrying a dead monkey.

The wig on the "woman's" head, clammy-brunnette as it was, had reminded me of the armpit-hair of that poor monkey, clotted with stale blood as it was. And, to put it delicately, that was the only thing on that "woman" that was mammal. The rest of her was sheer artificiality and vocal cords. She wore a see-through blouse, but on seeing through it, all I could decipher was a body that looked like the floor of a chemistry lab, and a pair of breasts made in East Berlin (I had to read the trade mark a second time to believe my eyes), a decided improvement on her eye-lashes which were stitched in South Croydon. I dreaded what one might discover the further south one scanned her abdomen. Perhaps one might find out too late that, after the ordeal of unbuckling and pealing off her skirt, there was literally an iron-cotton waiting to be crossed, a contingency which might necessitate the use of a passport to delve her secrets of Eve, not to mention "periods" of nervesluicing diplomatic de-frostization to usher in the "detente." To say she is a classic case of "Black Skin White Mask" would make Frantz Fannon have an erection in his grave because "Black Skin White Mask" is a state of mind which presupposes the existence of a Black Being underneath the White mask which, in this case, would be a total abuse of truth. Anything black or human within that carcass of creepy fiction has long been whittled away by self-imposed tyranny of post-colonial decadence. She spoke a language which was phoney cacophony of English, French and heaven-knows-what-else (I had not been warned she was multi-lingual as well). Her pet subject was herself, her pet hatred the "war." She blamed it on the "war" that she had not already got her Ph.D. at the record age of 22. She blamed it on the "war" that she had not already proceeded

31

to Paris to "mix with my type." She blamed it on the "war" that she could not escape from her black skin fast enough. Her academic career might read like something out of the diary of W.E.B. DuBois, I thought to myself, but she has yet to learn from the old prophet that the cause of war is the preparation for war. She blames everything on the "war," except the fact that she was the cause of the war. And, if unchecked, would start the next one. Baby, I pass ...

MOONDANCE

Asaba is a beautiful town. The River Niger lives there. I was invited a few days ago to attend the second funeral of the grandfather of a family friend. I arrived 24 hours late, and had missed most of the traditional extravaganza which my hosts particularly wanted me to see. But I had not regrets. My compensation was bountiful enough. The beauty of the place conquered me. If Asaba town had been human and female, I would have proposed marriage on the spot. And I would have named our first child, "Free."

The Midwest Hotels owes its beauty, not necessarily to its architecture, but mainly to the spot where it squals in modest serenity like a queen. It was a sublime surrounding. I couldn't hide my love for it. How can you hide a forest fire, I ask you. Because visitors and guests had to come by road, the hotel was constructed to turn its back on the River Niger. Which was a pity. Because, for me, this side of it was by far lovelier than the front. The river stretches into the distance like a flat field. A boundless blue sky joins it at the vanishing point, hiding there the infinite mystery of the universe. Silence is freedom, I said to myself, and apologised at once to myself for interrupting the freedom of this silence. They say that half of one's life is spent in dreaming. And perhaps that is why life is so sweet. Perhaps it is so dear because not everything one dreams of comes true. As I looked at the blue sky above, and then at the Niger doing the moondance in a silk of blue, I wondered why happiness is so unequal in this world. Why must each person have his and her own fate? Why must happiness be the twin brother of inflation? Why must lice consume grass, rust consume iron, and lies consume the soul? Why must God use the good ones, and the bad ones use God?

Two huge mango tress stood outside the hotel. The aroma of ripe mangoes fluttered in the wind like the flicker-

33

ing flame of a campfire in the sea-breeze of the night. I inhaled lustily. A little girl called Matilda was there with her young brother, patiently waiting and picking mangoes plucked by the wind. The boy was doing all the running and picking, while Matilda busied herself drawing with a piece of stick on the white sand.

Suddenly I wanted to paint, I could not explain it, but I could not help myself. The urge was powerful, irresistible, urging, urgent. And I wanted to paint, not on a canvas, not on paper, but right there on that white sand, next to little Matilda. My thoughts went back to a little Coffee House in Earls Court, London, called the "Troubadour." It was only a small place, two minutes walk from the Underground Station, but it had become famous because the basement was the meeting place of writers, poets, artists, and all tomorrow's people. I made many wonderful friends there, and a few weird ones too. But I remember one in particular, a young psychedelic painter called Mike. I can never forget our first encounter. I was in the Troubadour having my coffee when this bearded man walked in, and gave everybody a Yiddish salute, even though he spoke with perfect Irish accent, but was, in fact, Welsh. Then he kissed the chair, combed his hair with the fork, and sat on the floor. Then he dug his ear with a toothpick, whispered something in all seriousness to the leg of the table, selected a lump of sugar from the saucer, spat on it, and, with his best smile, offered it to me. I returned the smile with as much calmness as I could muster, shook my head, and told him politely that I wasn't hungry. I found out later that he wasn't being awkward or offensive. Mike was simply doing his thing. His inspiration came that way. By watching people react normally to abnormalities. But then he would walk home to his studio to paint, not people, but poetry. He specialised in painting poetry. Since poets were the first to use the word, surrealism, Mike felt, it was only logical that the summit of surrealistic experience was for the surrealistic artist to paint poetry.

34

As I knelt down on that Asaba white sand, next to Matilda, I felt as if Mike was leaning over my shoulder, and was pleading with me for old time's sake to paint his favourite poem. Though I will call my painting the Moondance, the actual poem is titled, "The People Speak", by Carl Sandburg. And this is what it sounds like:

"The people, yes, the people,
Until the people are taken care of one way or another,
Until the people are solved somehow for the day and hour,
Until then one hears "Yes but the people what about the people?"
Sometimes as though the people is a child to be pleased or fed
Or again a hoodlum you have to be tough with
And seldom as though the people is a caldron and a reservoir
Of the human reserves that shape history . . . .
Fire, chaos, shadows,
Events trickling from a thin line of flame
On into cries and combustions never expected.
The people have the element of surprise . . . .
"The Czar has eight million men with guns and bayonets.
Nothing can happen to the czar.
The czar is the voice of God and shall life forever
Turn and look at the forest of steel and cannon
Where the czar is guarded by eight million soldiers.
Nothing can happen to the czar."
They said that for years and in the summer of 1914 . . . .
As a portent and an assurance they said with owl faces:
"Nothing can happen to the czar."
Yet the czar and his bodyguard of eight million vanished
And the czar stood in a cellar before a little firing squad
And the command of fire was given
And the czar stepped into regions of mist and ice
The czar travelled into an ethereal uncharted siberia

35

While two kaisers also vanished from thrones
Ancient and established in blood and iron-
Two kaisers backed by ten million bayonets
Had their crowns in a gutter, their palaces mobbed.
In fire, chaos, shadows,
In hurricanes beyond foretelling of probabilities,
In the shove and whirl of unforeseen combustions
The people, yes, the people,
Move eternally in the elements of surprise,
Changing from hammer to bayonet and back to hammer,
The hallelujah chorus forever shifting its star soloists.
The people learn, unlearn, learn,
a builder, a wrecker, a builder again,
a juggler of shifting puppets.
In so few eyeblinks
In transition lightning streaks,
the people project midgets into giants,
the people shrink titans into dwarfs.
Faiths blow on the winds
and become shiboleths
and deep growths
with men ready to die
for a living word on the tongue,
for a light alive in the bones,
for dreams fluttering in the wrists ....
Sleep is a suspension midway
and a conundrum of shadows
lost in meadows of the moon.
The people sleep.
Ai! Ai! the people sleep.
Yet the sleepers toss in sleep
and an end comes of sleep
and the sleepers wake.
Ai ai! the sleepers wake! ....
The storm of propaganda blows always.
In every air of today the germs float and hover.
The people have the say-so.
Let the argument go on.

Let the people listen.
Tomorrow the people say Yes or No by one question:
  "What else can be done?"
In the drive of faiths on the wind today the people know:
"We have come far and we are going farther yet." . . . .
  The people will live on.
The learning and blundering people will live on.
  They will be tricked and sold and again sold
And go back to the nourishing earth for rootholds,
  The people so peculiar in renewal and comeback,
  You can't laugh off their capacity to take it.
  The mammoth rests between his cyclonic dramas . . . .
The people is a tragic and comic two-face:
hero and hoodlum: phantom and gorilla twist—
ing to moan with a gargoyle mouth: "They
buy me and sell me . . . . *it's a game* . . . .
sometime I'll break loose . . . . *"*
  Now the steel mill sky is alive.
  The fire breaks white and zigzag
  shot on a gun-metal gloaming.
  Man is a long time coming.
  Man will yet win.
  Brother the earth over might yet line up with brother:
This old anvil-the people, yes –
This old anvil laughs at many broken hammers.
  There are men who can't be bought.
  There are women beyond purchase.
  The fireborn are at home in fire.
  The stars make no noise.
  You can't hinder the wind from blowing.
  Time is a great teacher.
  Who can live without hope?
In the darkness with a great bundle of grief the people
  march.
In the night, and overhead a shovel of stars for keeps, the
  people march:
    Where to? what next?
    Where to? what next?

37

MEETING AN OLD FARMER

An old farmer asked me the other day:

"Tell me, Son, what do those European whites across the mighty sea think of us black sun-breeds down here in our lush African greens?"

To tell you the truth, Mazi, I replied, they think we are a people without a future, that we are a divided people, that we fight each other all the time, that we shall know neither greatness nor unity because nothing good comes out of broken debris and confusion.

At first, the old farmer looked stunned and seemed lost for words. But suddenly he beamed, and there was a mountain of wisdom in his eyes as he did what he did next. He dipped his hand in a basket of old grains, took out a single seed, gave it to me and said:

"Take this seed home with you, Son, and make sure you sow it before sunset tonight, in a mound of earth where it would be awash with sunshine and fine rain. Come back in exactly five days' time, the dawn of the next Eke Market Day from today, and tell me what lesson nature has taught you about the laws of growth. Let me tell you, in prediction, exactly what you'll find. At the first sunrise, you'll open the earth and find that your seed is disintegrating into pieces. At the second sunrise, you'll open the earth and find those pieces still disintegrating to yet smaller pieces. At the third sunrise, you'll open the earth and find that everything has disintegrated to dust.

At the fourth sunrise, you'll open the earth and find there nothing at all. This is usually the golden dawn of the prophets of doom. When the prophets of doom will tell you, as today, that all is lost. But just you wait. Don't despair, Son. Because on the very next day, as the golden sun heralds the fifth sunrise, it will also unfurl the seed-flag of a new miracle before your very eyes. Because out of that disintegrated seed, out of all that debris of confusion and seed rot, a beautiful young plant will emerge, shooting new life into the air with the smile of a new dawn. Such are the ways of nature, my Son. A beautiful flower grows out of the confusion of the compost heap, even as a new babe grows out of the staleness of the womb. And so it is with this land of ours today. This Africa of ours. This Nigeria of ours. What you now witness is confusion before construction, ignorance before knowledge, death before resurrection, sunset before sunrise, the fourth sunset before the fifth dawn of true salvation.

You can speed it up, or slow it down, but you can't stop it, Son. So I wish you the blessing of the gods on your way to tell the people of the town how a village greybeard feels about the tomorrow of this land. Get over that last hill before the darkness of this fourth sunset makes the hill unclimable for you. Maybe even you will live to see the new dawn, and hear the cock of history crow the dawn of the great fifth sunrise ahead."

The old farmer tightened his loin-cloth, picked up his hoe, and went back to his work. And I went home to ponder his words of wisdom with my other self.

MEETING THE FATHER OF MAN

I had a dream last night. And in that dream, I saw a wise old man with the face of W.E.B. DuBois. But his beard had grown longer and grey, tinged here and there with the greenness of eternity, and glowing over that domy head of his, which was also grey and tinged here and there, with the greennes of eternity. Illuminating the misty duskness of dreamland and time was a ring in the colours of the rainbow, which I recognised as the halo of wisdom, and also a mark of the Prophet.

Tell me, Wise Old man DuBois, I said, men have said many thousand things about you, some good some bad, but there is one thing they are all agreed upon: that your pen had on it the finger-prints of a god, the rumble and flash of thunder and lightning, the beauty and iridescent mellowness of Shirley Graham DuBois, your wife, and a wisdom which has made wisdom synonymous with W.E.B. DuBois. Tell me, Wise Old Man DuBois, you undieable dear little Big Man, tell me the secret to the magic of your genius, tell me what is the secret of great literature?

And the Wise Old Man looked up and said:

"A great writer, like the child he is, must only be heard and never seen. For power is in the hands of the assassins of Truth, and they will not hesitate to butcher him to prove to him they're not butchers. I say like the child he is, because a great writer, like a child, must begin life by lifting the veil from his eyes. And who but a child will spend the rest of his days combining the ever-enquiring mind of a child, with the near-masochistic dare-devilness of a child, with the lightning growth-fluidity of a child, with the painful loneliness of a child, with the invigilated veracity of a child, with the unsoiled intellectual virginity of a child, with the imaginative elasticity of a child, with the insane addiction to sanity of a child, with the self-appointed-God simplicity of

40

a child, with the expensive indifference to material poverty of a child, with the near-death-wish flouting of authority of a child, with the selfish craving for immortality of a child, with the insatiable lust for questions and answers of a child, with the re-tooling-the-ancient propensity of a child, with the spoilt-brat-yearning for the attention of humanity of a child, with the shock-absorption potentiality of a child, and then season it all with the wisdom of the second childhood of man!"

When the old man had finished, a divine smile lit up his beautiful halcyone face, a smile ten thousand years young – I beg your pardon! a smile agelessly young – a smile of artistic wizardry which will never know death, young, ever-green, eternal.

"Thank Goodness, great writers never grow old," I mumbled in my sleep. And as I woke up, I noticed I had lost a wrinkle in my sleep.

PART TWO

RETROSPECTIONS

KALIMA

The thirst for experience has driven me to many lands. The thirst of an answer to the question: Why do men suffer? Novalis has hailed suffering as the prerogative which distinguishes man from the brute, a token of high estate. I thirst to understand why this must be so. I thirst to understand who I am, where I am, why I am. I thirst for an introduction to myself: the strangest stranger I know. I thirst not to reprimand my fellow-man, but to recognize my share in his guilt. I thirst for, not the forgiveness of others, but my own forgiveness of myself, the only hope there is for the salvation of all humanity through pain. I thirst for some sort of higher spirituality and religion which the world has not yet known. I thirst for the day when Beauty shall be the religion of all men. Yes, I thirst for the impossible. That's why I am possible. Humanly possible.

A writer's life is hell. A writer is a one-man band of angels. A one-man crew of Lucifers. A one-man family. A one-man university. A one-man compost heap. A one-man traffic junction. A one-man jazz of ecstacy. A one-man choir of blues. A one-man man. Everybody's nobody. Writing is the loneliest occupation in the world.

Like Pablo Neruda of Chile, the writer today thinks of the entire earth and pounds the earth with his love. He does not want blood again to saturate mankind's bread, beans, and music. He wants all humanity to come with him, the farmer, the miner, the little girl, the lawyer, the seaman, the doll-maker, the trader, the engineer, the soldier, to read his works, to explore the literary jungles of his mind, to go into a cinema and come out to drink the reddest wine, the wine of the soul, of purity, of vision, of salvation, of resurrection through agony and self-forgiveness, of Godliness after conferring with the devel. This is no easy task

45

for the writer, to bear the cross of the despised, to be crucified for this, to be the voice of the unheard, to be spat upon for this, to be the eyes of the sightless, to be stabbed in the back for this, to speak the dreams of the unfree, to be deprived of his own freedom for this. Yet the writer plods on and on. Like all true people's artists, he must continue to aspire to touch the hearts of all men, whether they walk the high way of kings, or tread lowly the path of peasants. In short, his life must be a declaration of faith. Yes, it is indeed a life of hell. But I must admit that, once in a long while, it can bring a rewarding moment which compensates for all the other agonising moments which one has lived through. One such rewarding experience is the subject of this story.

Not long ago, I was invited to a neighbouring African country as a guest of the Ministry of Information and Culture. Naturally, I accepted the invitation, not just as a personal honour, but as a great tribute to African writers of my generation and a recognition of the role which we are expected to play in the great task of continental reconstruction which we have inherited. But what awaited me there was more than an honour, more than a recognition, more than brotherly embraces. It was one of the most thrilling experiences of my entire life.

To discover that my official host, the Minister of Information, was a homely young man, intellectually exciting, and as keen to put me at my ease as I was to communicate the purity of my intentions, in fact to discover that among the exciting writers I met were young men I could relate with, mostly under the age of 30, it was a staggering reaffirmation of my conviction that one does not have to be a Methusella to graduate in literary wisdom. It was a welcome change to be in a country where everyone, without exception, is sober 24 hours a day. Alcohol was totally banned. Everybody fed reasonably well, dressed well, housed well. More attention was paid even to the nutrition of the mind. Since the greatness of any society depends on the kind of individuals that society produces, it did not surprise me that people responded to love.

46

The hotel, where I was quartered, was like something out of Fairy Tale, a massive, dreamlike, building squatting on the slope of a hill, overlooking the sea. From my window, I could see straight down into a park, so alive with flowers, so atmospheric and so beautiful that the only time I recollected ever feeling so elated was in the lovely town-centre Plaza of Santa Fe in New Mixico.

One day, as I looked through my hotel window into this street below, I thought I saw something like an apparition. It was a bewitching vision in black silk. One glimpse as it moved in the gentle breeze suddenly reminded me of a graceful isolated black cloud in a setting sun. Before I knew what I was doing, I was already racing down the steps, propelled along by some mysterious forces beyond my control. However, when I got to the pavement outside, I was disappointed to find that the apparition had disappeared. Into thin air. I turned right, she wasn't there. I turned left, it was same. I ran to the top of the hill, it was no use. I ran down to the bank overlooking the sea. All I saw was a young fruit-seller arranging giant-size red apples on a movable horse-driven cart. I felt rejected, and then decided to return to my room. But just as I was approaching the door, something made me turn once more to look into the park. And there she was, quietly poised on one of the park benches. My apparition!

I approached her in trepidation, furiously practising how to say my opening lines. However, my fear was unnecessary. The young lady was very friendly. Life suddenly seemed all perfume. The wind jived in the sky, and the distant sea-shore became awash with sunshine. It hadn't rained for days but curiously enough, everything smelt of rain and young grass. I recited in my mind the saying: "God gave us memories so that we can have roses in December."

Some white birds flew across the sky. Where had they come from? Where were they bound? They did not answer me. They were calling loudly at something with cries so consistent and insistent it sounded like scolding.

The young lady's name was Kalima. She was from an

47

old Hausa family. But she explained to me with a smile that her black silk costume was not really Hausa, or even African, in origin. It was in fact Maltese, and the proper name for it was "ghonella." I reassured her that, African or not, the costume looked delicious on her. I have never been totally convinced that women always prefer platonic admirers. But there was something about this girl which made me feel she could be a rare exception. Her beauty was classic. Her skin was as brown as a Malasian. A voice whispered in my soul that here was a beauty I must be contented to worship from a distance. I wanted to be amused, but I couldn't. I read somewhere that life is only a comedy to him who thinks, but a tragedy to him who feels. I wasn't thinking. I was feeling. But it was a lovely sort of tragedy. And I found it curiously enjoyable.

The more Kalima and I talked, the more I marvelled at her spiritual expansiveness. Her belief in the destiny of Womanhood. In the brotherhood and sisterhood of all mankind. She was the first totally liberated woman I ever met. I thought this a little ironical because the African woman is generally considered to be the least liberated woman in the world. Kalima laughed at this, and dismissed the myth with a wave of her small hand. She said it was a matter of definition. Liberation is a state of the mind, never to be confused with Depravity in those social structures where Man has forgotten the proper use of the human body. Equality has always been a sanction of God. A final proof, Kalima recited to me a religious quotation where God, addressing Himself to men, says: "Live with them (women) on a footing of kindness and equity." And also: "The best among you (men) are those who are best with their wives ... Only he who is worthy of respect, respects women, and only the unworthy man treats them badly."

Kalima' face glowed with calm dignity, wisdom, and beauty as she spoke. She was certainly a girl of many surprises, I said to myself. But the greatest surprise of all came when I suddenly saw, for the first time, the white stick in her left hand. Then it registered. Kalima was

48

indeed blind. It was impossible to believe, because her eyes looked normal, black, seductive and alive like moist pebbles. It was a miracle. A girl who could not see with her physical eyes had managed, through self-education, to be able to see so much with her mind. I grabbed her arm and kissed her hand. And squatting down, I also kissed the ground she walked on. Any land that can generate so much sense of liberation in today's world in a person who is not only female, but blind as well, deserves every kiss of adoration it gets. Goodbye my black Sister, wherever you may now be. A beautiful girl without sight might be like a stringless balalaika. But I who thirst for the day when Beauty will be the religion of all men, also dream for a time when men will judge a balalaika by its inner tune, not its cosmetics.

THE PROFESSOR'S WIFE

One day, this story will become a book. I know they say you must never tell a dream, or it will never come true if you do. But I don't consider this a pre-revelation of a dream. For me, this is merely a sad little obituary. A gentle plotless lament for an old friend, who just passed away. One day, I will find a plot somewhere in the bizarre complexities of the situation, develop the theme into a book, and I will call my dream novel:"BLACK, BEAUTIFUL, AND BETRAYED." Meanwhile, all I intend to do this morning dear Reader, is to introduce you to one of the most fascinating characters it has been my lot to meet in many journeys through life. Hmm.

Hanover is a little American University town in New Hampshire, about three hours drive from Boston. A typical New England town, as they say, having only one main road, one post office, and one cinema. An enchanting little plateau. But what I will remember it for always is not its more famous features, like the Connecticut River, or the Green Mountains of Vermont, or even the White Mountains to the north and east. No. What I will always remember the town of Hanover for is a beautiful little drinking house called "The Green Lantern." It is a tiny sort of cottage situated on the slope of a hill. The place has an atmosphere all its own. Benign. Beamy. Calm. Spellbinding. Like something out of a fairy tale. I adored the place. Truth told, I was strongly tempted to call this story. "The Green Lantern," out of homage to the little pub. But I decided not to, for very personal reasons which I will not reveal.

Let me just say that it was here that Ilahi and I used to retire for our quiet drinks in the evenings. Ilahi was a petite, huge-breasted, warm, dark girl from Persia, who had the most devastating pair of eyes in the world. Every time she looked at the band, the lead-guitarist played the wrong key.

50

And when ever she turned those mesmerising eyes in full action on me, I simply went berserk with delight, and I felt as I could fly and fly and forever sing songs of joy for young lovers all over the world, like the Parakeets of Paraguay. Ilahi and I had met at the University Freshers' Welcome Dance, a real night to remember.

She was by far the most beautiful girl in the place. Heaven knows what she saw in me, but our friendship dated from the moment we clapped eyes on each other that night. But the tragedy was that Ilahi had already completed her course of Dartmouth College while I was only just beginning time. She had only a few days left to stay in America. Then she would board her plane and fly home to Persia. Since it was clear from the start that our Parakeet symphony was ordained to remain unfinished, we decided it was advisable not to start it at all. We were quite philosophical about it, parted good friends, swapped warm wishes, and said to each other it was a small world.

But Ilahi's departure ushered in real beginning of our story. Because before she left, Ilahi made me speak to her landlady on the phone, and I promised to visit the landlady and her professor husband the following weekend. What I did not realise then as I made this telephone promise was, however, what was really in store for me.

I will never forget that first meeting. Ducks were paddling in a little pond outside the house. A woman, as white as a pebble, no longer young, but cool and serene in a long seagreen dress, a red rose in her hair, was leaning against the door smoking a menthol St. Moritz cigarette. She held the cigarette in a long gold holder which she kept sweeping to her lips in poetic movements of her hand. At first, I though she was watching the ducks. But she wasn't. Her large blue eyes were riveted on the country lane where a little spaniel and a white cat were chasing grasshoppers.

The breeze wafted freely over the flowers in the garden, caressing the woman's face, making her eye-lashes dance in the wind. It was evident she had been standing there for a while. This made me feel guilty, because I was late. The

51

agreed time of my coming was nearly an hour ago. And I said to myself that, if I had realised that the woman was so ravishingly beautiful, I would have kept the G.M.T., and not the O.A.U. time, as I did.

Then she turned and smiled at me. That was when it happened. My heart stood still. I had seen this woman before, I said to myself, I knew that face well. Too well. But where? Where had I met her? Then, suddenly, it clicked. It dawned on me like magic. Yes, I recognised her. I was transfixed. I made the sign of the cross, not to invoke God, but to dispel incredulity. I found it hard to believe that this was really happening. Happening to me, of all people. If anyone had told me a week ago that this very moment I would be standing face to face with this living legend of a woman, I would have kicked the person in the mouth for talking such arrant impossibility, for living in the clouds. I rubbed my eyes to make sure this wasn't another one of my dreams, an apparition, a product of some mental aberration. But no. It was real all right. Such luck only came once in a life time. She really was there in front of me. Lunalisa, the incomparable Hollywood Film Star, in person. Lunalisa had been called many exciting things in her time: divine, supreme, elegant, unique, tantalizing, sizzling, sphinx, one-star glaxy, not to mention the world's most beautiful woman. This was a long time ago of course. I was still a child when she was already reigning as the queen of Hollywood. Then, all of a sudden, she disappeared from the scene. Nothing heard about her anymore. I often wondered what became of her. I was beginning to think she was dead. But now, look. What a resurrection. Look at her. Just look at her. Clearly she was well past her peak. She must be over forty now. But it really didn't matter how old she was. She still looked sensational.

I was so intoxicated with her presence that I was startled when a male voice spoke from inside the house. It was her husband, Professor Morrow, welcoming me. Sitting on a sofa, he looked well over fifty, and wore heavily lensed spectacles. A voluminous book lay upon on his lap. His

baggy trousers, brown shirt, maroon tie, and leather-el-
bowed jacket, was so off-beat, rustic, and so typically
English of his generation that it seemed a deliberate
caricature of the trans-Atlantic gulf between the Englishman and his American wife. He unclenched the pipe he was
smoking from between his teeth, waved it vigorously in the
air to clear saliva bubbles from the duct, and then motioned
me to sid down.

Here was a puzzle. What was a beautiful woman like
Luna doing with a man like this? They were the most un-
likely couple I had ever met. Utterly incompatible. She
was glamorous, graceful, vibrant, full of energy, and
dazzling like a pearl. What was this sexually-scintillating
flame doing with this balding, huggard, wobbly-kneed,
tired-faced, and retiring English intellected chunk of ham?
All this aside, he looked a hundred years older than her.
Why had Luna married this man? Why? She could have got
any man she wanted. What was their secret? What had
brought them together? What kept them together? To
complicate matters even further, they seemed to understand each other rather well. Even when they were poking
fun at each other, which they did often, they had a way
of making a visitor have, no illusions as regards who was the
outsider in the trio. They made the third party sense a sort
of impregnable secret bond between the couple. You also
wonder who was the real boss here? Luna? Or the uncom-
fortingly cool professor.

The answer to this riddle, and how I became Luna's
lover two hours after this first meeting, will be the subject
of my book. It will perhaps bring a few beads of perspira-
tion to the brow of students of involved literature, but I
think it will intrigue psychologists more.

I now feel free to write this story because I got a cable
yesterday, informing me that Luna died suddenly two
nights ago in a Hollywood hospital. She was the only person
on record who died of cancer, smiling. Even unto death.
Luna was a star undimmable. May her beautiful soul rest in
a heavenly cottage where she will find as much solace as I
found in the "Green Lantern." and beyond.

PEARL

I was coming back home to Nigeria. It was after a recent visit to France. I decided to make a brief stop in London to say hello to a few old friends. Among places I visited included a grave-yard. It is an obscure little cemetery in Western London where a part of me still lies buried till this day. If this sounds melodramatic to you, Friend, then all I can say is that you are luckier than I am, so lucky in fact you have lost nobody dearer to you than life itself. To tell you the truth, I am finding this story very difficult to continue. It is easier to write fiction than relating an autobiographical reality from your own tragic past, where every stroke of the pen is like a dagger stabbing at an old wound.

I have often asked myself what would have become of me if I had not met Pearl Prescod. One thing was certain. I would not have been a "writer" today. It is true that every writer has a Godfather or Godmother. Without encouragement from such a person, the author might not have the immense intrepidity and daring it requires to venture down the literary corridors where immortals like Shakespeare, Gogol, and DuBois have trodden, or the self-assurance and confidence necessary to make a career out of spinning dreams with a pen, like a woman who makes a living out of knitting sweaters from thread. However, to call this merely the story of my literary Godmother would be misleading. If it were that simple, there would be no story to tell, in fact. Pearl Prescod was more than a literary matron to me.

It began a long time ago. I was in London, lonely and alone. I live in a room, at Elms Road, and did my own cooking. For some reason, the English don't say "room", they call it a "bedsitter," which, in my own case, was apt because I was literally bed-sitting all the time. I would return from the Law School, lock my door, have my food, and then sit on my bed. When I wasn't reading, I was writing. Things

54

that gave other people pleasure, like alcohol, left me cold. I hated crowds, and felt much older than my real age. When invited to parties, I would find myself lonely, yet surrounded by people. The only thing I found self-fulfilling was creative writing.

Don't ask me how it came about. All I know is that I was always conscious of a nagging "presence" inside me. Deep down in my soul. Something alive and powerful. It has been there as far back as I can remember. Even as a child. Maybe before I was born. It was as if there were two of us in my mother's womb at the same time. Twins. Waiting to be born. Then one night, something happened like an internal lightning. My twin brother shrivelled under the shock. Became embedded inside me. We became one under my skin. He is forever asking me questions. Questions about the external realities of life which he cannot see from the depth of my soul where he is embedded. This dialogue is constantly going on between us. Of course I cannot speak aloud to him, because people will say that I am talking to myself, that I am mad. So I resorted to writing it down on paper. Sometimes what I write grows into a book. When it is a long question, the book is fiction. But when it is a long answer, the book is non-fiction.

The first thing I ever wrote was a play. I have forgotten what I called it, but it was terrible. It must have been 2,000 pages at least, and everything was wrong. Dialogue was as impossible as characterisation, and the stage duration of the play would have been three days. To make matters worse, I wrote it under the disgusting pen name of Ben Benue.

Believe it or not, it was this shocking script that I had the effrontry to take to Pearl Prescod. She was a world-renowned actress and singer, originally from Jamaica. I even rehearsed my speech. I was to make it absolutely clear to her that the copyright was mine and mine alone. All I wanted her to do was to read the script for me, her only reward being a vague hint of a promise from me to consider her for a part during production. Hmm.

55

She owned a beautiful house in Cambridge Gardens where she reigned like a queen. I travelled by underground train and got off at Ladbroke Grove Station. I followed the direction she gave me on the phone and, after a ten minutes' walk, I was there.

When I was ushered into the house, I was so dumbstruck I forgot my speech. She was even more beautiful in real life than she was on the television screen or film. She wore a pair of black tights and white pullover, and oozed femininity through every visible pore of her skin. She was not alone. Her pianist, an Englishman, was seated at the piano, and it was evident they were in the middle of a practice recital. But she showed no signs of resentment. She introduced me as Mr. Ben Benue, and actually called me a Playwright. Already! I felt so elated I could have fought a dragon with my bare hands. It was a moment of glory.

The very next day, the phone rang. It was Pearl. She wanted me to call back at her house that very evening. I did. But I was not prepared for the surprise treat in store for me. She had prepared dinner for me. And the food was so good I can still taste it this very minute as I write. But this was only part of the treat. She had, in addition, specially invited top four writers to dinner: two English novelists, one French poet, and a Caribbean playwright, every one of them a name to conjure with on the London literary scene. It was one of the most inspiring evenings of my entire life. I didn't know which was more exciting, the food or the conversation. Pearl said that the dinner idea was to "launch" me, to make me meet other writers who started like me.

When the other guests left, Pearl asked me to stay behind so that we could discuss my script. She said she had read it three times. Her verdicts were two. First on the author. Secondly on the script. She pronounced me "full of potential," but she found the script "too much." See her choice of words? The script had enough material for at least thirty plays, she said. My mistake was that I was trying too hard. I must take it easy, take my script home, and give it a haircut. She then gave me her blessing and sent me home, full of fire and determination to succeed in creative literature.

I did not see Pearl Prescod again until eight years later. Circumstances had altered a lot. I was no longer Ben Benue, but Obi Egbuna. One of my plays, "Wind Versus Polygamt," had been chosen to represent Britain in the "First World Black Festival of Arts" in Dakar, Senegal. And guess who had been chosen to play the leading lady Prosecution Councel? Yes, Miss Pearl Prescod. But the funniest part was that she no longer recognised me. I had grown a beard, I was bigger, I was bolder, I was much more mature. No longer the puny hyper-shy little boy whom she was feeding and pumping with confidence nearly a decade ago. Besides, my name was now different.

My first impulse was to fall down before her in gratitude, introduce myself, and thank her for all she had done for me. However, I changed my mind. I decided to do it in a more dramatic way. I would wait till we came back to London from Dakar. I knew that BBC had already planned to present the play both on radio and television soon after our return. So my plan was to wait till after the BBC television production of the play. Then, with a little more money in my pocket, I would throw a special marathon party for dear Pearl. And at the height of this party, before everybody present, I would call for total silence and, in a brief speech, I would reveal my true identity to Pearl, kneeling down in pure gratitude before this great lady, and then leave it to other guests to do the rest with applause. I saw it all happening in my mind's eye. It would be so dramatic. The build-up, the climax, the applause. No scene in any play would better it. And Pearl, though the star of the drama, would find herself speechless for once.

I kept this plan in my head all though our stay in Dakar. Pearl and I were always together. We were like mother and son. And the more I understood this woman, the more endearing I found her. She was the most popular actress in Dakar. And she knew how to court the limelight. For instance, when our plane landed in Dakar, the airport officials asked Pearl to produce her passport. In reply, Pearl pulled up her sleeve, pointed at the skin of her black arm, and said: "My skin is my passport." Then she went down on her knees, and kissed the earth of "Mother Africa" with open lips. She was stepping foot on African soil for the first time in 400 years, when her people were first dragged away in chains of slavery to the faraway Caribbeans. The entire airport echoed with applause, which reverbrated into the pages of newspapers the next dawn.

Everything went well in Dakar, especially at the Daniel Soreno Theatre, when the vaults reverbrated to the echoes of Pearl's powerful voice.

When we got back to London, work started almost immediately on the BBC production of the play. However, on the third day of the rehearsals, Pearl suddenly launched a vicious verbal attack on Charles Lefeaux, the BBC Producer. She complained bitterly that the prints of the script were too small, too tiny for her eyes to read. Everybody present, including myself, was surprised, because the prints were the usual standard bold type. Big. Pearl became so irritable that the Producer decided to put off the rehearsal till next day. But on the next day, Pearl did not even turn up in the studios. We telephoned her place to find out if she had left home, and was on her way. The answer was yes. Pearl had left home. But on a much longer journey than we envisaged. She had died in the night from brain haemorrhage. Her last words were reported widely. She was ready and contented to die, because she had seen Africa before dying. Her life ambition fulfilled. As I visited Pearl's grave a few days ago in London, it still pained me to realise one fact. She died without knowing that the play which made her African trip possible was in turn made possible by the few words of encouragement she gave to an insecure young writer a decade ago. Rest in peace, Pearl Prescod.

If the Writers' Workshop can do for some young writers even half what you did for me, I too will die a contented person.

58

ANGEL OF THE MORNING

For me, it was the most beautiful experience since the creation of the universe. I was sitting under a tree, quietly surveying the world with cool bemused eyes as usual. A tiny fly buzzed over my head and dashed itself against a branch of the tree. As it lay flapping to death on my lap, I watched the tragic incident in a sort of intrigued sadness. Though the dead fly was only a tiny insect, I could not help being conscious of the fact that I was present at a funeral. But in spite of this deep-felt sadness and respect for the dead, I did not want to go to the other extreme of jumping to my feet to make a funeral oration. So I decided instead to lay back in silence, and spent the few moments of sadness in solemn philosophical meditation, on the subject of Death itself. I sat in this posture for a long while, motionless, just thinking. But after some time, I noticed that my eye-lids were getting heavy with sleep. Heavier and lazier and drifting slowly into the unconsciousness of sleep.

But suddenly, through this mist of sleepy haziness, I detected two dim figures in the distance. They were human, and were walking up the hill towards me. Gradually, it became clear that one was male, the other female. There was something distinctly familiar in their style of walk. For a moment, my heart stood still. I wanted to be certain. Could it be THEM? Really THEM? I kept watching in breath-taking suspense. They came nearer and nearer. And my eyes got larger and larger as suspicion grew into a certainty. And as if in confirmation, the man extended his arms in an erratic manner I knew too well, and shouted out my name. The accent was Brazilian and his voice was as husky as ever. His female companion too was as beautiful as ever, and her smile was still so infectious it was enough to make any man giggle at a funeral. Before I knew what I was doing, I was on my feet, delirious with excitement, screaming like a

59

mad man as I ran down the hill with outstretched arms to meet them. We fell into each others embrace and, for a few minutes, could not even speak. We just stood there, staring at each other, weeping like children for pure joy of our reunion.

But here, dear Reader, I think I owe you a little explanation. You have, no doubt, guessed by now that my visitors were two lost dear old friends of mine. But this is only half the story. They meant much more than that to me. The young man's name was Moses Camilo. And as I hinted earlier, he was Brazilian. And the young lady? Her full name, before they got married, was Marya Belbina Toussaint. But we call her Marya the Bell, on account of her bell-like voice when she accompanied Camilo on his guitar. She was not from Brazil at all. On the contrary, she was born in a small town in the northern part of Martinique, one of the Windward Islands. She was always fond of telling us the story about a curious incident which happened in the northern part of this island as far back as 1906. It was the blowing up of Mounte Pelee. The story was that, without warning, this mount had erupted into a volcanic rage. The result was that all the 6000 inhabitants of St. Pierre perished, except one man. And gues who that single surviving exception was? A man who had been condemned to die. Marya made up a song based on this story and, every time she sang it, tears mirrored up in her large beautiful brown eyes. Marya the Bell is the only human being I know who looks as ravishingly beautiful when she is sad as when she is gay. The only perfect beauty I have recorded in my Diary of Human Saints.

Camilo and Marya met in London many years ago, and fell in love almost from the very first moment they set eyes on each other. It was only a matter of weeks before they got married. But they had a problem. Camilo was a struggling author, while Marya was a nurse at a hospital in Tooting. Camilo did not earn a penny from his writings, which meant that they both had to depend for their living on Marya's meagre earnings as a nurse. This did not do at

60

all. They lived in a tiny flat in South Croydon. Money was always a constant problem. Camilo needed some spending money. Which meant that Marya had to give him some pocket money weekly. This in itself was already a heavy drain on her pay-packet. And with what little she had left, she had to pay the rent, maintain the house, and keep two adults alive in London. To anybody who has lived in London, the intensity of the agony does not need to be spelt out. It was hell for the poor girl. And she suffered in silence. The tragedy was that Camilo could have been a successful writer if he had wanted. He was a brilliant poet and novelist. A real genius. But he was also a stubborn one. He had written a masterpiece, his first novel, which he called ANGEL OF THE MORNING. It was, perhaps predictably, a fictionalised biography of Marya, his angel. It was perfect. But no publisher would touch it. They said they did not like the ending. It was too sad, a terrible indictment of society, and was therefore bad for the market. So they demanded a compromise. They wanted Camilo to alter the end of the novel. Camilo refused, and told them to go to hell. He preferred to die in hunger like a man than to live in plenty like a zombie. What he did not realise was to what extent Marya was suffering.

I too (as now), was also a struggling writer. So, it was inevitable that Camilo and I would meet. We became friends, and respected each other a great dela. We were always together. And people took us for real brothers. I became so close to the family that I knew the financial violence they were living through. To cut a long story short, I will now describe what happened the last time I saw them together in their flat in London.

It was past midnight. Camilo and I had come back from town. As we opened the front door, and walked down the passage, towards Camilo's room, we distinctly heard someone sobbing inside. It could only mean that Marya was crying. But when we opened the door, the room was in darkness. Marya was lying in bed, and apparently, was in deep sleep. A tiny ray of light had filtered through an opening in

61

the window-blinds, dimly showing she was wearing an old, badly-worn, and torn nightie. The room was only a small kitchenette apartment and, though tidily kept, was rather crowded with things.

A passing car suddenly drove by on the sidestreet outside, and a flood of light from the headlamps swept past the window as the engine zoomed to its loudest and fainted away once more, giving the flat a fleeting flush of extra illumination.

Marya got out of bed, yawned, as if she had been sleeping for hours. She switched on the light and squatting down, proceeded to light an old smelly stove to heat the cold room. She had not done it earlier because there was too little paraffin in the stove: She was saving it till Camilo returned. She lifted an old Chinese doll on the mantlepiece, took out a lone pound note, and gave it to Camilo. His pocket money for the week. A pound was all she could afford to give him today. Prices were rising. But not the nurses' pay. Like in most countries. Nurses had to suffer much. Yet received too little. And from that little pay, there had to be deductions for tax, insurance, everything under the sun.

Marya looked beautiful as usual. But something was dreadfully wrong. Her hair was long and shiny black as ever. But there were suddenly bags under her eyes, making her look thirtyish in appearance, even though she was still in her early twenties. It was evident she had been crying for hours.

Camilo took her to task. He demanded she must tell us at once what was wrong. At first, she said that nothing was wrong. But at last she broke down, and confessed the truth to us. She told it inbetween sobs of tears, and the story was long. So I will cut it short.

It happened in the hospital where she was working. For some time, many patients were complaining that there was a thief in that particular ward because many things were missing. Especially money. They suspected it must be a nurse. The Ward Sister decided to catch the culprit. So she laid a perfect trap. The thief fell for it and was caught. Yes, the thief turned out to be our lovely dear Marya. Poverty drove her to stealing. In fact, on that last occasion, she stole the money to buy herself a new underwear. She had only one left. And that last single one was so old and frayed that she could only hold it up on her waist with pins. But it became so frayed that there were no longer patches to stick the pins. The final straw was that it fell off her waist, down to the ground, in the middle of the road, on her way to work, that very day. So she stole the money to buy herself another pair. But the law is not interested in why crimes are committed. Only in how. So Marya was sent to prison. Camilo was also sent to prison, because he knocked down one of the police officers who had come to arrest Marya. I went to visit Camilo and Marya in their separate prisons several times. Not long after that, I left London and came back home to Nigeria. I wrote to them several times, and got no reply.

So, dear Reader, you can imagine my excitement when Camilo and Marya suddenly turned up here in Nigeria, as I sat under a tree, just like that. After we embraced each other, Camilo opened his bag and brought out his brand-new book, ANGEL OF THE MORNING. The book had just been published and was proving a best-seller already. Marya opened her own bag and took out a bottle of Champagne. They said we must celebrate the happy reunion, and the new book, with a bang. I grabbed the champagne bottle, opened it, and it made a big noise as the cork flew up into the air. POP!

... then I opened my eyes. I looked about me. I was still sitting under the tree. I had never got up, or even moved from the place I was sitting. I looked about me again, and up and down the hill. There was nobody. No Camilo. No Marya. I had no visitors. Then I realised what had happened. I had in fact fallen asleep and dreamt it all. It was all a dream. This made me all the more curious to find out what had become of my old friends, Camilo and Marya the Bell. So, the very next day, I got in touch with the Brazilian

Embassy in Lagos. It was they who told me the truth. What really happened. And the sad story was that Marya, in fact, died in prison. She had become so weak, both physically and mentally, that she could not cope with the rigors of the London prison. So, she was found dead one wintry morning in her prison cell. As for Camilo, he did exactly what I knew he would do. He decided that he would convert his Angel of the Morning into his Angel of Eternity. Yes, he decided to join his Angel in Heaven because, the moment the news of Marya's death reached him, he hanged himself in his prison cell.

Somehow, I still find it hard to believe that Marya the Bell would never ring again, all because she was too beautiful for the era into which she was born to chime. But I am resolved. If ever I save enough money to build myself a house, I will call that house the "ANGEL OF THE MORNING." For me, it will never be a house. I will forever call it a book. And though it would be the first book ever to be written with bricks, instead of words, it will be a literary monument that would never tarnish as long as there are angels in the sky.

BLACK CANDLE, RED FLAME

Toddlers Close was an L-shaped cul-de-sac about 300 yards from where I got off the bus. End of journey at last, I thought to myself. The introduction card which they gave me at the Labour Exchange was safe in my pocket. It gave me a thrilling feeling to see TINGWELL & PHOENIX SHEET METALS written in blazing red capitals on the roof of the factory at the T-end of the little road, just as it was described to me. This was going to be my new work place, if everything went well at this interview. Only a man who had been out of work for a long time, and I mean desperately out of work, would understand the joy I felt at that moment, like seeing a new moon at the end of a rainy season and life was all a song. I crossed myself and said a silent prayer in my heart, thanking God in advance for a successful first day at work. Christmas was only a few days away and I needed every penny I could earn.

I made my way straight to the Personnel Department and, checking the name the Employment Officer at the Labour Exchange had scribbled on my card, I asked for Mr. Charles Pickles.

I wasn't sure what I expected Mr. Charles Pickles to look like, but the man who turned up was a tiny little fellow whose legs were so arched that they looked like two halves of a broken bicycle clip. His exact position in the firm was hard to tell, but obviously his job included interviewing "unskilled" workers like myself. This made him the sole arbiter of my fate, his decision was final whether I got the job or not. I couldn't see him extending this role to more intellectual employees though, his accent didn't strike me as being la-di-dah enough.

From the look in his eyes when he arrived, he seemed as if he had just finished rowing with somebody.

"Are you the lad from the Labour Exchange?" he barked.

65

"Yes, sir." I gave him my introduction card.

He looked at it and surveyed me critically. Suddenly he whipped a tiny comb out of his pocket. I couldn't imagine what he intended doing with it. There was hardly any hair on his head, only a narrow strip around the edges, just above his ears. This didn't deter him. He combed up a few strands from one side of his head to the other, across the shiny-bald dome on top, and then flattened them down with repeated strokes of his thick clammy hand. Satisfied with this, he began to pace up and down, his brow knitted in thought. He stopped all of a sudden, and, looking me full in the face, he declared:

"Yes, I think you'll do."

"Thank you, sir."

"When can you start?"

"Any time you like, sir."

"Like right away?"

"Suits me, sir."

"Good. I can see from your card that they call you . . . er . . ."

I told him my name.

"I'm afraid that won't do," he said, shaking his head vigorously. "Too much of a mouthful. By the time I remember it . . . let alone say it. . . . I'll forget what I want you for in the first place. Oh no, sonny, we'll have to think of some other name for you. Something short and civilised, oh, no offence, mind you."

"Anything you say, sir."

"Let me see now," he said thoughtfully. Then he snapped his finger. "How about Clay?"

I shrugged my shoulders indifferently. Anything as long as I got a job.

"Come to think of it," he want on, chuckling, "you look like him."

"Like who, sir?"

"Cassius Clay of course."

"If you say so, sir." I was about to add: "We all look alike, don't we?" But I changed my mind.

66

"Clay it is then," he declared, frowning suddenly. "And now, Clay me lad, the formalities are over. We've work to do."

"Sure."

"But first, I must tell you about the job."

"I was just going to ask you that," I said.

"They told you at the Labour Exchange we're only employing you here as a labourer, I hope?"

"Yes, sir."

"Well then, there're three of you altogether in our labour section. Two really, because the other one is the fork-lift driver. But, unfortunately, you can't meet your two mates today. They're off sick."

"Er .... they said something at the Labour Exchange about overtime. They said you'll explain more when I get here."

"That's on Saturdays. You don't come in so early. You start 8, clock out 1, and that's your lot. Only half-day Saturday. Five hours overtime. Good, isn't it? Considering all you do is wash the toilets."

"Wash the toilets, sir?" I couldn't help the note of disconcertedness in my voice. Nobody said anything about washing toilets at the Labour Exchange. Mr. Charles Pickles must have noticed my disappointment too.

He bared his teeth, but not in jest. "Of course you wash the toilets," he snarled. "What else is there for you to do on Saturdays? There'll be no lorries here to unload. Lorries don't come Saturdays."

"And do the labourers have to wash the toilets, sir?"

"An important part of your job, me lad," he said with an air of uncompromising finality which seemed to suggest: "Take it, or leave it!" Out came the comb again. "And that brings me to what you're going to do today."

"Oh, from what you said, I took for granted it's a truck-loading first day for me, sir."

"No, you can't do any loading today. The fork-lift is being serviced."

"Er .... it's like this, see?" he began with effort "For

67

about a week now, ever since your mates, the other two labourers, have been off sick, the toilets have not been done. For one whole bloody week, the only water that went near them toilets was somebody spitting or pissing. The toilets are in a shocking state, and the Guv is going round the bend. So, Clay, me lad," he added, patting me matily on the back, "since there's nothing else for you to do today, I think you better go down there and get your teeth in them toilets. Stands to reason, donnit? Eh?"

He led me to a store-room on the first floor of the works where a boy called Jeff fitted me with gum-boots and rubber gloves. The trouble was they couldn't find my size, so I had to squeeze into a pair of dirty old boots one size too small for me. But, on the other hand, the gloves were so large and made up of so many holes, especially at the finger-tips, that they seemed fitted to let in more water than they kept out. With this equipment, plus a broom, a rag, and a toilet basin poke, I clocked in for work.

I did not have to ask my way to the toilets. The smell was guide enough. Passing through one of the workshops on my way, I noticed through the corner of my eye that three English teenage kids who were playing with a brand-new lathe machine, machinists they were called, had dropped everything they were doing and, looking at me with a mixture of contempt and pity, started talking to each other in whispers. When I turned and looked back at them suddenly, they quickly averted theiry eyes, and began manipulating the lathe with such fury that the foreman might have been proud of them. They burst into a pop song, with such jarring haste and disharmony that Jim Brown might have been strongly tempted to sue. One of them, still conscious of me, chuckled by mistake, but the other two soon shut him up by nudging him on the shoulders. Obviously, the boys knew where I was going and what was in store for me.

I found out for myself soon enough. Gasp of sheer terror escaped me as I stepped inside the toilets and, for a moment, could not move. I expected things to be bad, but

68

certainly not in the quantity it now stared me in the face. It began to register why the man at the Labour Exchange had told me that this company sounded desperate on the phone. They needed a labourer at all costs, only qualifications required being a pair of sturdy legs and hands that were not in a sling. Unlike the other firms, they went out of their way to specify that they were broadminded enough to welcome blacks as well as whites. I had never seen a toilet in such a state before.

I stood there, speechless, rooted to the floor. I looked at the spectacle before my eyes, at what I had to do or starve to death, and tears stood in my eyes. My immediate impulse was to drop the goddam broom there and then and split, never coming back. They could keep their job, their bread, and their shithouse. But it wasn't easy. The thought of crawling back to that prison cell they call my flat, and facing the same breadless existence, and tell my pregnant wife that she stood a good chance of bringing up her baby due in three months on the dole.

So, I swallowed my pride instead, tied a rag over my mouth and nostrils, and literally plunged into work.

I was there till 5 o'clock, the closing time. When the clocking-out hooter sounded, it was like sweet music to my ears. I felt such a sudden sense of freedom as I never experienced before. The wind laughed in the sky and the air smelt sweeter than sweet, as if I was beholding the heavens for the first time. I was like a man dug out of a heap of earthquake wreckage. I was covered in grime, and stank like an open-air latrine.

No one would sit next to me on the bus going home. I was that malodorous.

As I finally got off at my stop, the local St. Mary's mission bell was chiming evening angelus. 6 o'clock. I decided to step into the church for brief meditation, to burn a candle, maybe have a little chat with the Blessed Virgin, tell Her about my little baby on the way, and ask Her guidance about the future, before going back to my place to scrub the filth off my body.

I had hardly knelt down to pray when, without warning, I felt sick, doubled over, and vomited. But the strangest part was that, as I cleaned myself, I had a sudden strange feeling that I was no longer alone in the church. I turned and there she was, a grey-haired old black woman dressed all in black. How she got next to me in the pew without me noticing her was beyond me. I was certain I knew every black woman in our ghetto parish, especially women of that age; there were not many of them left. But I had never set eyes on this particular old woman in my life. It was clear she did not belong to this slum part of town; she looked much too peaceful for that. Peaceful black women always were a rarity in Babylon, and she certainly wasn't a tramp. A shudder went through me as our eyes met.

She gave me a toothless smile. I tried to smile back, but I felt so self-conscious I began to twitch at the corners of my mouth. I just couldn't put out of my mind the fact that I smelt like a mountain of rotting dung. I had no right, I admonished myself, to inflict such agony on this kind-faced motherly old black woman. I stuttered a few words of apology, got up to leave.

"Can't you bear the company of an old woman, son?" she said, still smiling.

"Please don't think that, Maam," I said. "It's not because of you I'm changing pews. No, not you at all. It's me."

"What about you, son?"

"You see, I've been doing a dirty job all day. Sort of plumbing job. I'm afraid, I still reek a little of the loo."

"You don't reek of the loo, my son."

"What?" Something about her expression compelled me to sit down again. "I don't smell of the loo to you, Maam?"

"Not of the loo, my son. You smell of fear. You smell of weakness. You smell of castration. You smell of cowardice. You smell of being too far from home. You smell of manure used to cultivate other lands except the soil of your fathers. You smell of two million sanitary towels. Yes, my son, you're a fine construction of manhood no doubt, black and beautiful as a tropical night, but you smell of death."

70

"Why do you say I smell of death, Maam?" I said. "I am not dead."

"No, Why then have you taken refuge in a grave-hole in the slum of the dead? Why then do you dance away precious time to the distracting sound of the maracas while voracious vultures devour you like the carcass of a pig? Why then do you grin like a skeleton that isn't even tickled and then fail to scratch where you itch? Yes, my son, there are two million like you on this island, and you can't even raise a ping-pong team out of that number because the dead can't play ping-pong. Like the rest of them, my son, you died a long time ago. And like others have done before you, one of these days, you'll simply extinguish yourself with alcohol."

The more biting and penetrating her words, the more radiantly she smiled. Her eyes glowed with love and timeless wisdom, and seemed to be saying over and over again these unspoken words: "I know I've assailed thee with unkind words this day, but you've taken worse from others whose intentions were more ignoble than mine." I felt within the innermost fibres of my being that this old woman was translating into the language of my generation the eternal verities of the ages. Her words, from other mouths, might have stabbed me through like steel, but coming from her as they did, they caressed my soul with edifying mellifluence, like something out of the diary of a Mother Superior.

"Is there no hope for me then, Maam?" I asked. "Is there any chance of resurrection for men as dead as me."

"Go home, my son, and ponder over my words," she said. "Then and only then will you realise, that men were to resurrect in the past only when they stopped asking others if resurrection was possible."

Strange woman. I wanted to ask her some more questions, but she suddenly thrust a 5p coin in my hand.

"Do me a favour, will you, son?" she said. "Go up to the altar, put this coin in the box, and burn me a candle."

"With pleasure, Maam, with pleasure," I said.

I went up to the candle rack near the altar, slotted her

coin, and lit her candle. When I turned, the old woman had gone.

On my way out, as I walked down the steps of the church, I found myself wondering why no one ever thought of making black candles. Black candle, red flame.

THE SAD STORY OF SISTER BLUE

I am a simple village woman. I can't read, and I can't write. But a good many women would like to exchange places with me. And I have yet to meet a man who can walk past me anywhere without gaping. Because I am beautiful. Really beautiful. Young too. And clean. At eleven years old, I was already a spell-binder. A young man took one look at me and walked out of a Seminary. Imagine that! Just one look at my body gyrating to the rhythm of our village Nkwa-umuagbogho dance, and the poor boy walked out on God. To tell you the truth, I was more ter- rified than flattered. A tall tree is envied by the wind, as the saying goes, but there is a limit to how tall a tree can grow, especially when it means having God as a rival.

It was too much for a girl of eleven. At sixteen, I had become so lovely it was impossible to go to the village market without spreading dismay among husbands of homes soon to be broken. A school teacher once offered to murder his wife if only I would marry him. He was confid- ent that, if he produced me in court as the physical justifica- tion for his crime, any judge would acquit him on sight. I laughed in his face, and told him away with you. No judge would do such a stupid thing just for a woman's beauty, I said. I had been flattered many times in my young life, I laughed, but this one was tops. In reply, he simply shook his head, smiled at my ignorance, and told me that at some place called China, a woman's beauty ruined a dynasty. He could believe it now looking at me, he said, because my smile could split a mountain. This was too much. I left him and went straight to the mirror. I had to judge for myself. I took off all my clothes and stood in front of that mirror, to see myself as others see me.

Yes, there is no doubt about it. I am very beautiful. Even when not smiling, my lips part very invitingly in the middle, showing my ivory-white regular teeth. In the background is my dusky skin, black as a cloud, tight over my young full-blown breasts like sari over cones of volcano. My face is perfectly oval, a marvel of symmetry, adorned with a nose so perfectly placed and tapered that even Buddha would envy the structural equanimity of my face. And crouching over my head like a live panther is my hair, combed out tantalizingly in the style they now call Afro. I must confess with all due modesty that, studying my nude body now in the mirror, my bosom is entitled to all the adoration it gets from male admirers, not to mention the disapproving glances from envious women. I never wore any artificial gadgets to strap my bosom up or down. It was not necessary. Padding was even less necessary. Truth told, I used to think this part of my body over-developed. But I can see now that it goes well with the ample curves of my waist, two young breasts towering over my well-chiselled navel like two cones of a hill standing over a valley of gentle stream and vegetation. As for my thighs, the less I set your imagination on wings regarding them, the better. They tell me there is a saying about how two men looked through same prison bars, one saw stars, the other mud. In the same way, two people can look at this story, one will see the beauty I am describing, while the other prefers to ruin it from himself by injecting into it the ugliness already present in his dirty mind and then concocting pornography out of it all, and blaming it on me. I tell this story for the spiritual enrichment of all those who feel like that Russian writer called Anton Chekov, or so they tell me, who once described the human body as the holy of holies. It is my belief, though ignorant as I am, that God created and gave beauties like me to the world so that men can draw nourishment for their souls. The tragedy is that I am willing to play this noble role, but the souls of many men are not good at digesting nourishment, and seem incapable of touching purity without turning it into ugliness, sin, quagmire, in their minds. Suddenly nobility becomes ignoble, stale, a far echo from what it set out to be.

Nature made me beautiful, and put me in the most

74

picturesque village in the world. My story began here one sunny morning. We were on our farm, working. Myself, my mother, and my three younger sisters. My father had died when I was little, and I had to forget going to school. We all lived by working on our farm. Today, for instance it was dawn. The birds were singing, the palm trees were dancing, as the wind cooled our bodies as we perspired and worked.

Suddenly a car pulled upon the side of the road. It was a strong-looking car, a jeep of some sort, all covered with dust and mud, and doors plastered all over the mementoes which indicated the traveller had been to many lands. To our surprise, a white man came out. A strange looking white man. To start with, he was bald, not a single hair on his head. He was stocky, but not fat, and his nose was too towering and strong for a white man. His neck was full of folicles, and the rest of him was all muscles. All he wore was a pair of shorts (showed off his hairy legs) and a flowered shirt with a middle button missing. I can never tell a white man's age, but this man must be well over fifty, I thought to myself.

To my surprise, he walked past my mother and my three sisters and headed straight for where I stood. After watching me in silence for a while, a cry of suppressed agony escaped him. Suddenly he thrust his hand into his pocket, counted out ten crispy new Naira notes, and gave them to me. He didn't allow me time to ask what for. He simply and calmly told me to undress. Yes, to untie my wrapper. Just like that. The strange thing was that I was not even shocked. There was something kind and noble in his face. Something dependable, pure, and clean. It gave his unshaven rough face a sudden glow of beauty. I looked at my mother, and she nodded assent. I looked at the man once again, and for the first time he smiled. There was something Godlike in that smile. A smile of clean, uncorupt homage to beauty. Before I knew what I was doing, I was standing naked in front of this strange white man. He collected his equipment from the car and told me to stand still. All he wanted

75

to do was paint me. He said that I was the most beautiful woman he had ever seen in his entire life. His one dream through life, was to paint a woman like me. The wind laughed in the sky, the leaves danced in the trees, the birds sang a chorus of halleluya, while my sisters teased, chuckled, and giggled. I just stood there, looking irresistible. The man painted away. In ten minutes, it was over.

When he showed me the painting, I didn't know what to say. It was a perfect picture of me, but only the upper half of my body was revealed. The rest of me was ensheathed in roaring flame, and looked terrifying. When I asked him why, he told me to look at the title he had scribed at the lower end of the picture. I told him I couldn't read. Then he read it aloud to us. It said simply: "THE MADONNA IN HELL." Below that painting, was the artist's signature. A local teacher found that signature difficult to decipher. He only made out the word: PICASSO, or something like that.

That picture was no painting, I tell you. It was a prophecy. That painter was no artist either. He was a prophet. He saw through my fate at once and knew what life had in store for my. My life has been one endless hell ever since. I am not yet 30, but I have been married ten times. Each husband collects me into his household like an ornament, uses me till the novelty wears off, and then abandons me into the jaws of misery. They have used me like a child machine, to produce babies for them, and, like all machines, I have been reduced to a mere wreck. And the sad thing about the human machine is that it is the only machine that is not serviceable, that you cannot reactivate with spare parts, that you cannot rejuvenate with oil and borrowed energy. But I am resigned to my fate. I live now at Obiagu Road, here in the slums of Enugu town, earning my keep under circumstances I dare not disclose to my children. I tell the children in my letters that I live in a convent. What I do not disclose to them is that it is a Convent of Jezebels.

It is here that a writer called Obi Egbuna came to see me.

He said he wanted to publish my story on the first Sunday of March, at the launching of International Women's Year. I doubt if he will ever keep this promise. But if this story ever sees daylight, please remember, dear Reader, that I am a woman too. All man once told me in consolation that every harlot was once a virgin. One of the greatest calamities that could ever befall a beautiful woman is to be born in a society where men have no souls, and where beauty is not appreciated. Women are considered inferior to men, which is bad enough. Now put yourself in my position, dear Reader, I am a woman considered inferior to other women. Violence is not always accompanied with the boom of guns, the flight of bullets, or the flashing of bayonets. It can also mean the unspoken conspiracy of class distinction, not only imposed by men upon women, but more especially by women upon other women. By women in "God's" Convent upon women in my Convent of Jezebels. Both of which are man-made. And woman-made.

HAPPY ENDING

I am a hill. The war-gored city of Enugu is lying like a frightened invalid at my base. Right now, I can hear a Seminary Mission bell sobbing for the sins of the people. They call me Miliken Hill. I am half marble, half stone. I reside here in West African sunshine.

Today, I am old, a neglected old man, a little hunched at the back, with slopy shoulders, like an enfeebled giant, a decrepit anthill, with my lower valleys crawling with human ants. I call these people "ants," not in derision, but in admiration, because no animal in creation has more resilience than the ants. Try watching them if you don't believe me and you will soon find that, if you tear the net of a family of ants, they will start rebuilding it at once. Damage it a thousand times, and they will start all over again a thousand times, without taking a rest. That's the resilience of ants for you, and so can Man be too, when and where he wants. I have seen a lot in my time. I've borne this old city on my back all these years without complaint, and I love the people more truly than a father loves a toddling son strapped to his back. But like all toddling children, they've taken me for granted, so much so for granted they have almost forgotten I even exist. I know I am well past my prime, my inside palpitates with bilious quakes every-time lighting caresses my peak in flirtation. I am even balding on top, little by little, caused by those yearly harmattan cruel winds which are sharper than a million razor blades. But like all old men, I have been around long enough to be depended upon for one or two stories that could bring tears to your eyes. Let me tell you just one.

As you know, I have been standing here like a granite anthill from time immemorial. To many Christians, the spring of water which shoots out and flows down one side of my face has been put there by God from the beginning of time to quench the thirst of trekking sons of God. To thousands of Moslems, it has been installed there by Allah at the dawn of eternity to wash the feet of nomads on their way to graze or sell cattle down the hill. How wrong they both are! That "fountain" has in fact been tears of sadness or joy, which, as occasion moves me to do, I have alternately shed for the sorrows or salvations of those human ants down my base. Yes, I have seen it all.

I was here when the whites arrived, and here when they left. I have seen dark sons of the soil take over power and drop it like a pot of boiling oil, and what spilt over when the pot broke to pieces turned out to be the blood of their fellow sons of the soil. But the most terrible thing I've seen was the civil war, and I still have not quite recovered from the dents and scars of the bombs of that inferno. This is the crux, the cross, and cradle of my story. This is no place to describe the horrors of that war in detail, for every one knows what war is like, particularly that war. Besides, so many books have been churned out already concerning that war, not a single one of them accurate. For those who can give an accurate account of what really happened in that war are now rotting as skeletons in graves dug on my sides. And for another good reason, this is not really a war story. It is more a story of the tangents of sorrow that can grow out of war, and possible resurrection to follow.

Yes, I saw it all. I saw tribal emotions drummed up by grandiloquent outsiders whose purity of intentions were more ostensible than actual. This country became a theatre of inter-tribal blood-bath unimaginable in the history of Black Africa. Armed with weapons of destruction, brothers were set against brothers. I saw acts of killings, maiming, brutalising, dehumanising, butchering, and hate once undreamt of in this land. Cruelties were unleashed on a level these once-jolly people never thought possible in themselves. It was even carried into the womb of pregnant women where unborn babies were scalped. The poor toilers of these lands who had pain all their lives and quenched their thirst from the same streams suddenly became stran-

79

glers who drowned each other with waters of affliction. Men ate the flesh of other men in anger, and women were driven by hunger to vie with vultures for the carcasses of their own infants who had become victims of the war. One of the saddest stories was that of a seven-year-old boy whose body once lay at the foot of this very hill, cold and stiff. When his mother came for him, he was lying in a pool of his caking blood and vultures were already hovering over head. His skull had been smashed in by a bullet and the rest of him was also riddled with bullets. Even if he had lived, he would not have been able to call himself a man again, for one of the bullets had ripped off that part of his anatomy usually considered unmentionable in stories intended for the ears of both young and old. Yet only a few minutes earlier, this little boy was full of life, zest, and energy, just like any other boy in this battle-torn area of battle-worne people. A short while before, he was playing and running about gaily in the green fields, chasing grasshoppers in the glorious West African sunset, killing time and waiting for his mama to call out when supper was ready, to call out that it was time to quit playing in the fields and come home because "Deh-deh," the old papa who tapped palm-wine for a living, would soon be home, exhausted and starving as usual. But what the little boy did not know was that two plantoons of the opposing armies were silently closing in on both sides. Suddenly he was caught in the crossfire and, the next moment, he was dead. To call this a sad story is an understatement. But the saddest point of the story is not the manner of this boy's death, or that he died young, or even that he died at all. The real tragedy is that he died without knowing why. And in this, he was not alone. Hundreds of other children suffered the same fate that same day in other parts of the country, just as others did the previous day, and many more certainly did on the morrow's dawn. Peasants were also being slaughtered in thousands without count between every sunset and sunrise, the lamentable fact still being that none of them had a clue why he was dying.

All they knew was that they were full of hate, and the

victim of their hate had committed an unforgiveable crime. What was this crime? The man had been born on the other side of the Niger. Yes, it now sounds ridiculous in retrospect, but men had hated each other to the point of murder for no other reason than that. They were born on different sides of a river. The war ended, but not the hate. The hatred lingered on, in spite of genuine efforts by genuine men of government to fan down the ugly flame of hate. The evil wind of bitterness continued to blow through the land, no matter what. The hangover of distrust and disdain continued to distort and contort the soul of a once-happy people like a hangover of vampires after an orgy of blood. The more they hated, the more it became clear that what they felt was no longer hatred for their fellow men, but love for the idea of hatred itself. At one time, this reached a point where it became almost certain that the situation was beyond redemption, that all advocates of reconciliation were fighting a losing battle, that every generation began by laughing at the tribalistic foibles of the generations before it, and yet in the end followed a path which inevitably wound up in the very same abyss of hate. All seemed lost, yes. Till . . . one day. Till the day our story opens.

A young orphan girl from Udi was running away from a cruel master and madam. They had been maltreating her since she was a little girl, and she now felt she had had enough. She had set out all the way from Nsukka, and was heading towards Enugu. She was travelling on foot, not because she had underrated the journey, but mainly because she didn't have a choice. She had no money, not even a Kobo coin, to call her own. After the 9th mile to Enugu, she was forced by sheer exhaustion and hunger to fall down and sleep.

When she woke up, she discovered she was no longer in an open field, but in a tent, well covered with blankets. A pair of black eyes were staring down at her, and she woke up with a start. She wanted to scream in fright but, when she realised the beauty and kindness glowing deep down in those eyes, her scream trailed off into a shy chuckle. The eyes belonged to a young Hausa boy called Aminu. Born in Yola twenty-three years before, he had been walking cattle from one part of the country to another since he was six. To him, there were no boundaries among peoples, people were no pieces of geography, but just human beings. Even if they were, he liked this piece of female geography now in front of him, and the wind chuckled approvingly in the sky. The girl, in turn, fell at once for this young man who, for the first time in her life, served her a meal in bed, even though the bed was only of dry leaves, and his cooking could do with some improving. Two months later, they were married, with belly-bloated cows for bridesmaids. But it was a wedding to remember. Nine months later, a baby boy was born to them, and they called him Uche-Allah. Yes, you've guessed it, this was the baby-hero of our story, the baby who was the product of that marriage.

Why was he so special? Because in that little baby, what I saw was more than the birth of an infant, it was also the resurrection of hope, the communion of the Igbo and the Hausa on the altar of love, the burial of hate, the arrival of a new Nigerian, the first resonance of a happy echo from the past, the second Independence of a United Nigeria. That baby, needless to add, had its first wash in that fountain gushing down my face and, from that moment, what was earlier mere tears of sorrow for the sins of these people tearing themselves asunder, suddenly transformed into tears of joy for that first whiff of a happy wind, blowing down to the human ants down at my base, ants whose resilience is being proved once more that, no matter to what extent the microbes of history have eaten deep into their shelter of survival as a people, you can always count on them to come fighting back to rebuilt it with strength that emanates from love, maturity, and hope. For they know that, human nature being what it is, destruction may raise its ugly head from time to time but as long as hills like me (the old but defiant Miliken) are here, erect and intact, pillars and monuments testifying to the resilience of this multi-race as a people, the rest they can always build again.

82

LETTER TO A SISTER
(from London Prison Diary)

Dear Dolores,

I feel like writing you this letter because I am in remand-custody in Brixton Prison, London, and don't know what will become of me tomorrow. You have every right to tear it up, if you like, without reading a word. Had you done so already, I wouldn't hold it against you. But since you have started reading, I will presume you want to know what made me behave the way I did. I will therefore waste no time praising your nobility of spirit. To do so at this stage could easily be misconstrued as condescending and therefore fatal. But one thing you must know right away is that you are the most beautiful eighteen-year-old woman I have ever seen in the nude. This makes my action even more difficult to explain, but, unless you have this fact from the start, there can be no further dialogue between us. Unless you believe that what I did had nothing to do with any physical or moral inadequacy you might think you have, we cannot proceed. And we have to proceed, if not for your sake, for mine. We mustn't let them see our tears, must we, Dolores?

It was not until you ran out of the hotel room that night that the full implication of my action came crashing in on me. I suppose, had there been a third witness, this might sound an exaggeration, especially as you walked quite slowly out of the room, your head bowed, tears running down your face, your dazed figure dragging like a little girl some priest had refused absolution after her first confession. I watched you till the door closed noiselessly behind you. It was a quiet and unhurried retreat, but you and I know, as you alone knew then, that you were running as fast as your laden head would let you. It was not until later, much, much, later, that it dawned on me what agony you

83

were living through. And I wouldn't have known it but for the echo of your last words.

"I am sorry I have only succeeded in making you feel this way. I was only trying to be a good prostitute."

I tried to recollect how it all began. When I first set eyes on your face, I had recognised there what I had seen a thousand times before. I had seen it in the ghettoes of Washington and San Francisco, I had encountered it in Vine City, Watts and Chicago, I had witnessed it in Harlem, England's Brixton and Perry Bar. I first knew it in Port Harcourt, and later on, in Lagos and Senegal's Dakar. It exists in any corner of this earth where the peddlars of democracy have emancipated Black women to the level of peddling sex for a living. I call it the voidness of Ego or the Baptism of filth. They made you wear a mask, too tightly, too long. You had been playing a part all these years, so that even you had come to believe that that part was indeed you. They had made you sell your body for a living and, to forestall your only refuge, told you you were a "sinner" and therefore had no soul. They had called you "Miss Shame" and you had responded, "We sure is." This was what you were when we met, a self-confessing Miss Shame. And yet, within the two hours that led to that dreadful last moment, I watched you undergo a transition. The real you came out. It showed in your conversation, your laughter, your curiosities. You told me to hell with twenty dollars, with my writer's philosophies, to hell with God. Happiness glowed in your eyes as you danced around the room like a manumitted slave. I was flattered no end that I had something to do with your new-found freedom. I know I dismissed it as nothing at the time, but I was quite moved when you thanked me rather lavishly for being kind to you. I tried in vain to convince you that I was not being kind to you, period! That I meant every word I muttered.

Your two companions, the two white girls who were with you when we met, were no match for you in any way. They knew it, too, and their brashness, I though, was a wasted attempt, a desperate one, to contradict this fact.

84

I was irritated at the way the one you called Barbara had accosted me on the pavement as I stepped out of my hotel. Yes, I stay here, I replied. Yes, I am foreign, African, visiting from London. No, I am not a student. No, I do not want a woman, I want some chicken. Yes, at this time of the night I happen to be starving. Yes, yes, no, no, yes! She kept on and on. I don't quite know whether I did it to slight her, or because I was beginning to find the curious mixture of beauty, coyness and silence that was you more and more intriguing, but, if you remember, it was at this point that I shut her up by telling her I had changed my mind.

"Didn't someone say," I joked, "that a woman is like a chicken? Kill her and she supplies you with nourishment." But Barbara did not laugh when I ended up with "I most certainly do want a woman. That one!" And I pointed to you.

Poor Barbara! She was absolutely disgusted with me. Cautioning me that you were going to cost me twenty dollars, she turned to you with that patronising air of hers to remind you that you were expected to come straight back to the joint as soon as you finished with me, evidently you were supposed to account for every twenty-dollar earning you made to appease some Rachman of the sex world.

Let alone with you, I was at my wit's end what to do with you. You must have noticed my hesitation about rushing you straight into my hotel room just to have a twenty-dollar affair. I was grateful when you came to my aid by intimating you knew of a nearby restaurant which stayed open till dawn and where the chicken was good.

The summer night was cool and enchanting, but the wind moaned ominously as we walked down 48th Street. From halting exchanges, our conversation became speedier and less inhibited. We warmed up to each other so rapidly that by the time we got to my hotel apartment and finished our packed meal, you had told me all about your unhappy childhood, your mother's tragic death, and your miraculous existence. You told me more than enough to make even

85

the most hard-hearted of men fall down and weep. Yet I did not weep, not because I am a man of strength, but because the internal injuries my heart suffered from your sad retrospections were soon soothed by the sweet iodine of joy which your new animation sprayed into my soul.

I was uncommonly edified as I watched you undergo this self-induced process of ego-manumission. Like a flower at the dawn of spring, the real you unfolded and blossomed before my eyes. You became as free as air, having decided to forget, at least for the night, that even the North wind is still amenable to the laws of the North.

It was no longer the self-abnegating Miss Shame who now looked me straight in the eyes and smiled as if challenging my manhood to stand and live up to its task. Gone were your mask, your shackles, your veil. You had not a care in the wide world when you tilted your head to one side and asked me to take you in my arms and treat you like a woman. As you said so, you looked as if, all through your life you had been starved of all uncommercialised love. Kindness had been a foreign quantity till now and sex only a torturous gyration of the lower abdomen till twenty-dollars worth of animal friction had been cranked out of you by some inconsiderate blood-sucker, Black or White.

But today, tonight, this moment, your appetite for the first time in years, perhaps in life, was whetted, and all the feminine biological urges in you, hitherto dormant, were yearning for real masculine caresses. I understood your torment, and the necessity to complete what I had started struck me as urgent and logical.

At the time I gave you an encouraging nod, I was perfectly satisfied that all would be well. I watched you undress, watched you reveal with every strip, that my imagination had not exaggerated the beauty of your nudity. In his poem "The Black Woman" Marcus Garvey articulated his veneration for the beauty of Black women. As I looked at you, I felt as if a voice were whispering Garvey's words inside me:

86

Black queen of beauty, thou hast given color to the world!
Among other women thou art royal and the fairest!
Like the brightest jewels in the regal diadem,
Shin'st thou, Goddess of Africa, Nature's purest emblem!
Black men worship at thy virginal shrine of purest love,
Because in thine eyes are virtue's steady and holy mark.
As we see no other, clothed in silk or fine linen,
From ancient Venus, the Goddess, to mythical Helen.

The more I looked at you, the more my heart was ravished at the sight. When you bent down to tug at the lace of my shoe, I saw the line of your neck and the curves of your breast, and immediately I became drunk in your presence. Within me, masculinity panted away like a locomotive. The flesh of your breasts and thighs was dark and lovely as the night. I felt a certain desire to press close, to caress and love you till all your tantalising pliability was exhausted. I heard myself echoing your words, "To hell with twenty dollars, to hell with caution, to hell with God!"

It was then that I began to undo my shirt. But, as you well know, I had only progressed as far down as the third button when my hands stilled. Something seemed to have snapped within me as I stood there, silent, gazing unseeingly over your shoulders into space. Judging by reels upon reels of thoughts and ideas that raced through my mind, I must have been in that pensive posture for a long time. The next thing I was conscious of was your voice asking me if anything was the matter. And as I replied, my voice, though sounding as if it came from afar, was a very determined voice indeed.

"Put on your cloths, Dolores."

"What was that?"

"I said: put on your clothes."

"But—"

"Please don't argue with me. Just do as I tell you."

"If it is my friends you are still worried about, I told you not to bother. They can wait at the joint. I can handle them. Honest!"

"No, Dolores, I am not worried about your friends."

"Then it must be the twenty dollars. Don't you believe me? I don't want a dime from you."

"I know you don't. And I am flattered. But you must dress now. I am sorry."

"Don't you understand, I feel –" You broke off, held me close and began to stroke my neck. But your hands, a moment ago radiant with the heat of passion, had suddenly become as cool and impersonal to me as a barber's touch. Female intuition! You sensed how I felt.

"I see," you said despondently, relaxing your hold. You remained speechless and motionless and that old mask began to take hold of your countenance all over again . . . . You tried to hold back your tears, but a shiny drop fell to the floor. You apologised for soiling my carpet and then turned to put on your clothes.

Not long afterwards, you were gone. But not before you had made a brief halt at the door to sob those last unforgetable words.

"I am sorry I have only succeeded in making you feel this way. I was only trying to be a good prostitute."

I have stated more than once that it wasn't till minutes after you had left the wretched room that the full meaning of those words became clear to me. It was evident you had misunderstood me and misinterpreted my action. No doubt, you had taken me for a snob, a hypocrite who, in spite of my sweet words and superficial gloss, remained, when it cane to the test, a westernised Tom who would not share love with one of my own kind because I considered her morally untouchable, a pariah.

With words of seeming kindness, I had encouraged you all along to break out of the social latrine (to which you were at least partially resigned) and to cultivate self-respect, to stop being a twenty-five-hour-a-day harlot, a Miss Shame with a past and to see yourself as a young woman with a future and an ability to give and receive genuine love. But when, in spite of yourself, you began to react positively to my sweet sermons, and, indeed, the woman in you began to respond to the man before you with love that was far from illicit, I, the great preacher, could not bring myself to forget that you were a harlot. Seeing kindness and pity shining in my eyes, your keen imagination had approximated them to genuine respect and desire even to the point of love.

You offered to warm my soul with your body and, if necessary, wipe my feet with your hair. Only a woman in love could make such an offer to the man she loves. By flaunting that offer, I had proved that the only sensation I sought from your company was a titillation of ego which emanated from the contrast between your social position and mine. Whitey-defined social position!

These reflections saddened my soul. What made it most intolerable was not so much that you had thought me worse than I deserved, but the realisation that, if I let you run away with these wrong impressions, if I did nothing immediately to correct these odious notions, I had created more psychological problems for both of us than I had set out to remedy, considering your exceedingly sensitive nature. In a matter of seconds, I was resolved.

I bottoned my shirt and dashed out of the room in the hope of catching you before you went very far. When I got to the lift-stand, you had gone. What's more, all the elevators were in use. Waiting was out of the question. I ran down the steps, all the way from the seventh to the ground floor. People in the lobby looked at me askance as I jostled through them like a madmad. I ran into the street and searched everywhere. In vain. You must have taken to your heels the moment you found yourself at the other side of the door.

In desperation, I hurried down to the end of 48th Street, looked left into Times Square and right towards 49th Street. It was no use. You had disappeared. It was one of the most painful moments of my life. The more my mind dwelt on it, the more terrible I felt. I realised how stupid of me it was to presume that you would understand! And how silly to attribute the tears coursing down your cheeks to a gesture of sympathy with what was going on inside my head! And how can a girl fathom the mechanics of a strange mind? You hardly knew me! To misconstrue my motive was the most natural thing for any girl to do under those circumstances. And that was precisely what you did. Your reaction suggested it and your words revealed how soul-scathing it must have been for you.

My first impulse was to trace you to the address you had given me. I had to see you, if only to take back the dagger I had so unwittingly plunged into your bleeding heart. However, after I reflected on what you had told me about your "landlord" and the ethics of your profession, I decided to forget it. But I made myself a promise there and then: to write you this letter as soon as I got back to London. This, Dolores, is a fulfilment of that promise.

But, having decided to write, I am beginning to realise that the task is not as easy as I thought. To explain why I could not go to bed with you, I must first recount the last-moment thoughts which led to that resolution. To make you fathom the intensity of those thoughts, I must go back to my actual experiences in America, experiences that provoked the thoughts. And to help you appreciate my reaction to American society, it will be necessary to show you how history has moulded my reaction to the world. This means, of course, relating why I came to America, what I make of America, and what America has made of me.

This therefore is my task: to dissect the America that I saw, re-define the me that you met, and show you how you came to represent a culmination of a phalanx of historical forces which have been in operation since long before our time. Having done this, I shall leave it to you to assess the wisdom or the inevitability of my action. I am under no illusion however that, given the same circumstances, stronger men than I could not have handled the situation more impressively than I did. I must therefore ask you to bear in mind that, notwithstanding those romantic pictures you painted about me, you are dealing with no superman. You must remember that it is me and what history has made

90

of you and me, that you are judging not a man in a vacuum.

As for me, I am strongly what the times have made me. My English education has turned me into a tramp. Education, I was once led to believe, is like a slot machine: you insert a child at the age of five and extract him fifteen years later to find him well-educated, sure of himself, and free. The machine seemed to have broken down when my turn came. The conflict between what I expected to find in England – the White man's land where the machine is designed – and what I actually saw there has since driven me into a perpetual search for the truth. My lot has become tramping about the world, seeing things and people, sharing their dreams and nightmares, writing down my findings and, one day, laying me down and dying.

It was in this spirit that I flew to America from London. I embarked upon a journey which was to take me thousands of miles over the "New World."

For nearly two thousand years, European civilization has been based on the unhealthiest of social contradictions, that between a philosophy and religion which proclaim the brotherhood of man, and an economic structure which divides mankind into masters and slaves, exploiters and exploited, victimisers and victims. America, today, represents the epitome of this social misgrowth. The experiences of Greece, Rome and Great Britain notwithstanding, the United States of America insists on championing the cause of this contradiction inherited from Europe, even if it means the destruction of mankind. Writes Dr. W.E.B. DuBois in the *Battle of Europe*:

> *The civilisation by which America insists on measuring us and to which we must conform our natural tastes and inclinations is the daughter of that European civilization which is now rushing furiously to its doom. This civilization with its aeroplanes and submarines, its wireless and its "big business" is no more static than that of those other civilizations in the rarest days of Greece and Rome. Behind all this gloss of culture and wealth and religion has been lurking the*

world-old lust for bloodshed and power gained at the cost of honour.

My first confrontation with militant Black youths was in Atlanta's SNCC Head Office, an unfurnished, dilapidated grey building in the stenchy slums of Vine City.

I saw them in their police-scaring revolutionary outfits, jeans, threadbare old clothes and overalls, as they worked from dawn till midnight, or often into the early hours of the morning. They were mostly young people, some just out of college with impressive degrees, a good many still in school, a few who simply left school because the White man taught them nothing there that could improve the plight of the Blacks. Their spirit of dedication, hard work and organisation was incredible. With the possible exception of Messenger Elijah Mohammad's Muslim Mosque in Chicago, I cannot recall anywhere else in the world having come across such a tantalising collection of beautiful Black women, all without exception wearing their hair in the "Natural Look." They told me the secret of their beauty. Hard Work.

We discussed Black grievances as we toured the offices. The Negro, they pointed out, is physically separated from the Whites in the United States. What the Blacks now want is a psychological separation which will allow the Whites to destroy themselves. Harlem is more compatible with Mozambique in Africa than with any White community in the States. SNCC has been striving for Black political power in areas which are predominantly Negro, but this has been frustrated by Whites. 1965 Arkansas was a case in point. Eighty percent of the population was Negro and the authorities rigged the election, claiming that the ballot boxes had been lost. One of the main aims of the SNCC go-to-the-people offensive was to encourage the Negroes to go to the polls, while the Whites' counter-offensive was to create a paralysis of fear and let the Black masses know they have nothing to lose but their nightmares.

The country is racist, they said repeatedly, and it doesn't

take much to prove. The White man has been given "one more chance" once too often. The Black man no longer believes in one more chance for the Whites, because it means less and less chance for the Blacks. They believe there is a patent connection between the situation of the White world outside and the racial happenings within America. To counter this effectively, Blacks of the world, 500 million strong, should separate into one unit, build their own economy and civilization. Whether they recombine eventually with the White bloc would then depend on whether the Whites develop from their present level of cut-throat animality to the level of civilised human beings.

To date, Integration – physically, politically, and cultur-ally – has meant the attempt of Blacks to move into White neighbourhoods, paying for their thwarted efforts with their own blood. This is no coming together of equals, which is what Integration should be. Till the economic basis for genuine equality amongst all peoples is laid, all talk of Integration is a fraud. The tragedy of the Black man is that he has been a victim of this fraud too patiently, too peacefully, too long.

So that I should see for myself, they decided to walk me through the slums of the ghetto to the SNCC business office at 142 Vine Street. It is hardly credible that a place with a name as romantic as Vine City should turn out to be the very entrails of Hell. The streets were broken, sparsely tarred, and pock-marked with ditches. Old shacks squatted alongside the streets like curious squashed match boxes put together by some pack rat builder with a sick sense of humour. Here and there these "houses" were patched with rust-eaten car bonnets in place of glass windows – the cold had to be kept out somehow.

I saw Black men and Black women, citizens of the American affluent society, crouching on doorsteps like little animals, chained to their pillars of poverty by ever-thickening cords of discriminating Yankee capitalism. Some of them strolled about aimlessly as if it were a public holiday. Jobs were scarce; they were non-existent. Young women, who under different circumstances would have been paragons of beauty, sauntered along the street, battered and worn by the degradation of the one ready job, prostitution. Beneath their eyes, lines of suffering plastered over with cheap talcum powder were nevertheless visible, like little worms smothered to death with a paste of araba ash. You could easily tell from the "high" look in their eyes that they had indeed learned to smoke.

On one corner of the street, hemmed in by shacks, was a little rough clearing which was supposed to be a children's playground. Even that, I was told, had been a recent innovation generously introduced to improve the lot of the kids. And as I watched those pathetic half-naked children running on rough gravel without shoes, I wondered if they knew what the future held in store for them. Indeed, the slums of Vine City, like the slums of Harlem I was to discover later, were a lamentable testimony to man's inhumanity to man, and this was in a country which professes to go to the faraway Vietnams of this world to prevent Vietnamese inhumanity to other Vietnamese.

At one point, as we came to a rise at the end of the street. I looked into a distant White area and saw a new Pentagon-like skyscraper shooting up into the heavens as if to mock the poverty-stricken ghetto dwellers of Vine City.

"What building is that?" I asked one of the boys. "What will they do with it when it's finished?"

"I don't know, brother," one boy replied with unnerving quietness, "But I can tell you one thing for sure. That goddam house ain't gonna stand there for long. I have a feeling somebody's gonna mow it down with dynamite real soon."

"Yeah," the rest joined in, and began to chant in growing frenzy, "Burn, baby, burn!"

I was relieved when the night finally came and they took me to the hostel where they all lived like dauntless crusaders. After I had changed into my African national robes, they treated me to the most moving reception party of my American tour. Forgetting all the trials and tribulations of

94

mankind for a few hours, we wined and dined and guffawed and sang revolutionary songs about Lumumba, Nkrumah, Odinga and Black Mother Africa. This was all the more significant to me because I had been warned before I left London that the Negro in America totally dissociates himself from Africa and looks down upon everything and everyone "African." In my experience, however, for the average Afro-American family to have an "African" visitor home for dinner was something akin to a status symbol. Not only did they implore me to come to dinner in my national costume and give the invariably packed party a "back to Africa" touch, they even insisted on my coming to breakfast if all my dinner times were already booked for the period of my stay.

It was in the early hours of the morning that I returned to Peach Tree Hotel. As I lay down on my bed, pondering my experiences of the past hours, it was all too clear to me that the fun had ended with the last echo of laughter and that, with the approaching dawn, I would once again be wading through the realities of the worst Hell on this earth, the Hell of the American deep south. And even that is only a slice of the truth. For the whole of America is the Black man's Hell.

And even that is not the whole truth. For America is also the Red man's Hell.

My visit to the Indian Reservation in New Mexico stirred the innermost fibres of my being. The fact that the original settler of what is now America has been squeezed into a position where he has hardly a place to lay his blanket is an impression which will remain indelibly in my mind as long as I live.

I can still hear the quiet voice of the Jemez Indian Chief counselling me with all the reserved dignity of a king. "Never let anyone take away your culture from you, son. Because once it's gone, you'll never get it back."

He was a little old sage with intelligent, laughing eyes, and he received me in the sitting-room of his red adobe bungalow. Though he was small in stature, his presence was

95

overwhelming. His clothes consisted simply of an ordinary cotton shirt, tight long pants and a red band around his head. This was how he remained except once when we posed for a photograph. He rose, threw a folded red blanket over his shoulder, placed a regal, embroidered leather medallion around his neck, and held his royal sceptre in his hand.

Otherwise, reserved and withdrawn, he sat quietly till he had listened to my explanation of the purpose of my visit. After scrutinising me carefully and weighing my every word, he was disposed to talk and chatted most amiable without losing his fatherly deportment. Those who think that Yogi Maharishi Maheshiogi is the sage of the age should go to New Mexico and meet Paramount Chief Picos of the Jemez Indian Pueblo.

Making me sit on the sofa beside him, he answered all my questions with quiet dignity, telling me all about the internal administration of his pueblo, the history and philosophical attitude of his people and the cultural and religious ties between the people of his peublo and seventeen other pueblos in New Mexico, the attitudes of his people towards America and the "modern" world generally, and his personal dreams and visions of the future. I marvelled at this man's knowledge – and who will blame me after I had seen for years the Holly-wood portrayal of American Indians. I found plenty of love in the Indian way of life, and certainly a great deal to learn from it.

I was there when a burly-looking Indian youth came in and, seeing from the chief's countenance that his presence was unwelcome, thrust something into the old man's hand, bowed respectfully, and walked out again. When the young man had gone, the chief unclenched his hand, displaying a thick wad of dollar bills. Apparently the young man had smuggled a bottle of liquor from his place of work in the city into the pueblo and been caught in this unforgiveable infringement of the pueblo law. The elders, under the chairmanship of the chief, had sat in judgement over this man, found him guilty, and levied a fine of thirty-five dollars on him. That was what he had come in to pay.

"I never allow alcohol in this compound," stated the old man with grim finality. "And as long as I am the governor here, I will never allow any white man's bad habits to infiltrate my compound and deprave my people."

I left the Jemez Pueblo with plenty to chew over in my mind. I went away resolved never again to listen to anyone selling me the idea that the American Indian is a self-immolating xenophobe whose life is founded on war dances and an inherent aversion from self-improvement. I carried away the horrifying picture of what Africans could easily become if pig-headed politicians continue to sell us out to those traditional bearers of the White man's burden whose God-given duty is to castrate non-White natives all over the world.

I met White Americans who, with not uncharacteristic flippancy, explained away the Indian Reservations as the White man's painful duty to respect the Red man's wish for undisturbed isolation. But they never told me that this isolation, supposedly so respected, so sacrosanct, so undisturbed by the Whites, is negated when they draft the Red man into the White man's army to fight the White man's battles.

We hear about the Red man's aversion to modernisation, when the truth is that no people on this earth will reject modernisation and industrialisation unless that "modernisation" seeks to destroy the culture which it professes to strengthen. People are reluctant to accept "modernisation" which, in fact, threatens to subject their culture to another culture which they consider alien and inferior to their own.

Like every visitor on a cultural tour of the United States, I never ceased to hear about the Red man's reluctance to change. I saw the evidence of this "reluctance" while I was there. Yes, I saw it in Indian-owned cars, bicycles and modern lorries driven all over the pueblo; I saw it in Governor Pico's colour television set and the forest of television aerials growing over the pueblo roof-tops; I saw it in the Indian's willingness to send his children to city schools in Alburquerque – and saw the White man's unwillingness to open wide the gates of knowledge to these "reluctant" people. Instead, Indian children are herded, apartheid fashion, into a seprate school of their own for fear their inherent inferiority might rub off on White children and lower White standards.

"The native does not want to mix!" White Americans say with eagerness. It is not without a familiar ring. You hear it in Australia. You hear it in Canada. You hear it in South Africa. You hear it loudest today in Zimbabwe. You hear it in any part of this world where a handful of greedy Whites are preapred to destroy human values by lying, cheating, distorting history, and profaning defenceless men in order to lay their hands on the property of their victim.

"I have no spur to prick the sides of my intent," moaned Shakespeare through the lips of Macbeth, "but only vaulting ambition, which o'erleaps itself and falls on the other," Shakespeare knew his people well.

To contemplate the sufferings of the American Indian is disturbing enough. To go there and actually see this suffering against a background of magic, the splendour and the beauty of the surrounding Indian country is simply unbearable, like watching a wingless new-hatched fledgeling preyed upon by white ants.

I stood there and watched this magnificant expanse of Indian country till tear drops stood in my eyes. I have seen beautiful spectacles in my life countless times; I have stood amidst the white hills of tropical lyiegbuoma back home and watched the sun set the way nobody else knows it in the world except the select villagers of Eziora; I have kept vigil on the banks of the great Niger and watched the tides come and the surfs doing the silk dance; I have stayed awake at night drinking "illicit" gin and watching the stars dancing over the blue lakes of Olu Jungle while wild cats howled away in the distance and half-naked brown women breastfed their cooing babies in the moonlight; I have travelled to Senegal and made love to the most beautiful woman in

98

Dakar while her husband was outside the door, sharpening a hatchet rather noisily on a grinding stone and asking the servants within my hearing distance how thick my neck was; I have trekked all the way up and all the way down the majestic spirals of the legendary Milliken Hill of Enugu Coal City while the cocks crowed in the dead hours of the morning; I have even retired like a hermit to the cave zones of Holywell Bay to drink in the beauty of nature in the serenity and wizardry of Cornwall's undiscovered far country; but never before in my life have I been so cowed, as I was that day, by the bewitching majesty and magic of the New Mexican Indian country.

Towering up with pyramidal elegance were countless mountains, white hills, black hills, red hills, indigo hills – all colours of the rainbow – jutted out like the fantastic Mountains of the Moon in a splendour far beyond the powers of poetry to describe. To see all this fluorescing between a setting sun and a rising full moon was enchantment itself. No wonder, I gasped, the Indians fought so hard to keep this earthly paradise to themselves. The sky was a miracle of cloud formations, the landscape so vast and peaceful that there was no need even for the trees to grow too close together – and didn't they know it!

Miles and miles of beautiful country stretched to the horizon. Everything here seemed larger than life. One soon begins to understand the simplicity and humility of the Indian life and religion. For who can gaze at Stupendousness itself, for centuries dominating this vast landscape, without being quailed into the acceptance that man is but a tiny insect crawling about on a little pond-holding rock called Earth.

From Albuquerque to Santa Fe I roamed, and from Santa Fe to Los Alamos, climbing mountains at dawn and dipping into moon-drenched sulphur springs at night. It has been said that the first White man went to New Mexico in search of the fabled Seven Cities of Gold. Later generations followed in search of silver, oil and uranium. Some have gone purely in search of solace, rare in the cut-throat

99

jungle of the North. I, probably the first African tramp to arrive, had gone there simply in search of the truth. And, in spite of the bitterness of the truth I found, I went away resolved that if ever I decide to retire and die in some serene isolation outside my native town of Ozubulu, it will be to New Mexico that I must surely return.

Flying out of New Mexico and into California was a different story. It meant the end of a perfect honeymoon with spiritual bliss, and the beginning of another voyage within the racial chamber of horrors America calls The States. Los Angeles is a special case. Everything she does, she does with a vengeance. She evokes the greatest glamour and produces the worst scum; she makes top millionaires overnight, and topples twice as many into bankruptcy in half the time; her dream is Hollywood, her reality is Watts. Here the Whites hate the idea of integration almost as keenly as they love the practice in bed. And the Negroes, who began by hankering after both the idea and the practice, have ended up being betrayed by both.

I was in a barber's shop in Watts one day when the barber thrust a little booklet into my hand. As I turned through the pages, my eyes caught a poem by Jack Markham called Imminent Hate." I remember this poem particularly, not just out of professional interest, but because it reflects both the mood of the Negro in the ghetto and the Negro's attitude toward religion and God at this time. I reproduce this poem here because nothing I write as an outsider could reproduce the mood with more clarity and feeling than this Afro-American has. He was obviously verbalising the innermost convictions of his heart, a heart which, whether one approves of it or not, is the heart of the now Black America, a vital force in the history of the new Third World, the force that must decide the future course of mankind by forcing the White world of power into imminent confrontation with itself:

You'll make us hate you yet, I fear,
You dominators of the Earth,

100

For you say you're right when you know you err,
And you robbed us gradually, from birth.
Although the facts of your history
Are recorded by you with pride,
My God, Religion, and Nationality
Emerge as vague bromides.
You told us God was in the sky,
And the ultimate was heaven's street,
But do you seek the Sweet Bye?
No! You're ever robbing me at my feet!
And too, the women depicted up there.
The angels so blonde and white,
Why, I'm afraid to succumb to Pearl Gate,
You might lynch me on sight!
Religion might be a virtue inducer,
And man's guide to the stars,
But if I meet you – (Excuse me Lord),
I'll detour on to Mars!
"Love one another" in spite, you said.
Turn cheek, both right and left,
If soon I don't rest my paining slapped head,
I'll be tempted to kill myself.
The physical slavery that we did see,
Under you for three hundred years,
Gave you time to distort our history,
Oh! The rattle of chains in my ears!
You kept us away from schools and books,
And raped our women as you pleased,
And lynched us by reason of only "one look,"
Your derelictions have never ceased!
Oh, that joyous day when the slaves were freed,
Their eyes were aglow,
Too trusting to know they had been deceived,
They still wore the stigma "Negro."
How long do you think I'll be pacified,
With a vision of heaven's street,
A job yet to find, a pint of wine,
And a History that doesn't speak?

This was the language and mood I was to encounter from now on as I tramped the Black ghettoes of America and delved into the soul of the grassroots. It was the mood of Watts in Los Angeles; it was the mood of the Philmoore District in San Francisco; it was the mood of the Black Bottom in Detroit, it was the mood of Central Avenue in Cleveland; it was the mood of Sower Street in Philadelphia; it was the mood of 47th Street in Southside Chicago; it was the mood I met, ate, drank, slept and chimed blues to in 125th Street, Harlem; it was indeed the Negro mood. In fact, in a book actually called *The Negro Mood*, this was how my friend Lerone Bennett, summarised it:

> Less than *one hundred years ago, Nietzsche announced to a startled world that God was dead. Religion apart, he was announcing a psychological fact, the death of God in the heart of his contemporaries. What we have to deal with today is a psychological fact of a similar dimension. The white man is dead. He died at Auschwitz and Buchenwald. He died at Hiroshima. He died in Montgomery and Birmingham and Little Rock. The white man is dead. Men with pale skin still live. But the idea of a man with a certain color skin and a mandate from God to order and regulate the lives of men with darker skins; that idea is dead—in Panama and in Kenya, in Milwaukee and Mississippi. We no longer live in a world controlled by that idea, though some people, Negroes and Whites, have not read the obituary notices.*

But the one man who had read this obituary notice long before Lerone Bennett was a man known to the world as Elijah Muhammad, Messenger of Allah, leader and founder of the American (Black) Muslims. My meeting with him in his home in Chicago was without doubt the highlight of my American tour.

The incidents which led to that meeting were in themselves remarkable. The previous day I had attended the Muslim Service at the Temple of Islam No. 2 in Southside, Chicago. I arrived a little late and was stupefied to see that everyone present was immaculately groomed in a dinner suit and black bow tie. And the Muslim Guards,

102

in their blue uniforms and star-studded round hats, looked like a regiment from a superior planet. They were tall, handsome, and very disciplined. In my casual dress –simple sports jacket and grey, tight slacks, I looked like a real Teddy boy in their midst.

With their unfailing polite smiles, the guards told me nicely but firmly that no one, not even an invited guest like myself, was allowed into the temple not properly dressed in a dark suit. This was in accord with Messenger Elijah's aim of making the Black man respectable. To expect respect from others, you must communicate respectability. Elijah's law, they said, could not afford to be a respecter of persons. I saw their point, especially as they offered to provide me with a car and driver to take me all the way back to Manor House Hotel, wait for me to change into proper attire, and bring me back again to the Temple in time for the service.

More curious than ever, I accepted the offer and, in less than half an hour, was back. They escorted me straight to a reception room in the Islam University block adjoining the mosque. Here I was welcomed by one of the "Brothers" with the same customary disarming politeness and smile. He gave me a form to fill in but, for some reason, insisted that he write the particulars down himself while I dictated the necessary information. It was soon plain that literacy was not his forte. Apart from the difficulty of printing the letters one after the other laboriously till a word was completed, when he got to the dotted space for my profession, he printed in bold letters "RITER." I had nothing but respect for this lean, ageing man when I found out that until a month before when he had been released from jail, he had been totally illiterate. Not only had the Muslims cured him of drug addiction, thuggery and slow self-destruction, they had in one month's time instilled into him enough self-awareness and pride for him to transform and dedicate himself to a life of spiritual guidance to others less fortunate in order that they, too, could follow the same road to self-education and nobility of spirit he himself had trod.

The Muslim "Sisters" milled around like a band of

103

angels, clad in immaculate white robes and long head tunics. Their faces, dusky and beautiful like a bevy of Nefertitis, glowed through the white wraps like the sombre lustre of the setting sun. Spiritual contentment and love shone in their eyes as they welcomed new members into their fold. That disarming Muslim smile, the first thing one notices about these Muslims, looked even more infectious when radiated by the girls. At first, I wondered whether they were pulling my leg. But I soon became engulfed by the sheer force of their genuineness. There was something about the presence of these Black Muslims, even when I was in the company of the most formidable man alive, Muhammad Ali, which made me feel that, for the first time in my life, I was meeting real human beings. With the Muslim Sisters, this quality seemed even more pronounced. They wore no make-up, displayed no phoney airs, no artificialities. You can therefore imagine the awe of everyone present when a youth, looking at one of the "Sisters," suddenly declared:

"Isn't she a witch!"

"Man," cried his friend, horrified, "you are crazy. What did you say a thing like that for?"

"Baby," came the reply, "only a witch can go about producing this paralysing effect on people just by parting a pair of lips in a smile."

The role of the Negro woman in the Black revolution is something which has fascinated me for some time even long before I went to the States. From the outset, the Negro woman in America has always enjoyed a privileged position compared to her male. The Whites have always preferred to integrate with her when confronted with a choice, and have given her a job, even if only mopping the floor, while her husband stayed at home, with wounded pride. In this way, the Negro housewife has come to be the accepted breadwinner and, consequently, the esteemed boss in the household while the husband's authority has been virtually whittled down to nil. Potentially, therefore, the role of the sexes have been reversed in the Negro household and, on a com-

104

munal level, the Negro women have come to constitute a new class of white-collar workers.

With the emergence of the new Negro revolution, therefore, the Negro woman is in a dilemma. Must she now join hands with the Negro male and fight the very White man who, after all, has given her the privileged position she enjoys, or is it wiser to ignore the noise of battle and, with the indirect support of silence, help the Whites sustain the status quo in which she has vested interest? Must she join the Negro revolution and help bring about the liberation of Blacks, male and female, or is it more sensible to use her privileged position to be the vanguard to a world-wide struggle for female emancipation, Black and White? Is she woman first and Negro second, or Negro first and woman second?

I must say I was moved by the sheer energy and devotion of the Muslim girls, who had obviously made their choice. They had chosen to stand by the fathers of their children and champion the cause of revolution which, with proper ideological orientation, must surely be the beginning of the end for those who want to keep the dispossessed permanently dispossessed, male and female.

At the mosque entrance, I was handed over to a band of Muslim guards for another routine preliminary prior to going into the Temple. I was searched from head to toe. Sill wearing their customary smiles and making small talk (Have you been long in Chicago, sir. . . . Do you like it? . . .), they left no pocket unturned, no article unexamined, no part of me unsearched for concealed weapons. That was how, I was told afterwards, they came to discover on one occasion that a male visitor had three balls between his thighs, one of which turned out to be a hand grenade. Yes, it was a thorough search, to say the least.

The search over, they apologised most profusely for subjecting me to this treatment and hoped I would appreciate why no one could be rated above suspicion – their enemies were mighty and plentiful and would stop at nothing to blast them out of existence – Allah knew they had tried and would try again IN VAIN.

At long last, the gates of the Temple yawned before me, and with the voice of Minister James 3X thundering from the pulpit in front, I stepped inside . . . .

The next morning, I was woken up by a rather early telephone call, at 6.30 a.m.

"My name is John Ali," a voice said at the other end. "I am the General Secretary of the Muslims. We met yesterday after the service, with Muhammad Ali."

"Yes, I remember you well," I replied.

"How would you feel about meeting the Messenger of Allah himself, Mr. Elijah Muhammad?"

"I would love that very much," I replied.

"Mr. Muhammad has said the pleasure will be his." Note the choice of words. "He requests you to be his guest of honour at dinner in his home tonight."

"Splendid. Tonight suits me fine."

"I'll pick you up at 5.25 p.m. at the Temple."

I was a quarter of an hour late but John Ali was patient and smiling, as if being kept waiting was a treat for him. We went into the Islam University block from the front and, going right through, emerged into a sidestreet where a car was waiting. From there we raced to Mr. Muhammad's Hyde Park home. John unlocked the front door with a special key of his own and led me straight to the bathroom to wash my hands according to Muslim custom.

As I stepped out of the room, I felt a hand touch me on the shoulder. I started and turned.

"My name is Elijah Muhammad," said a little man standing before me. He took my hand in his, shook it with fatherly affection, grinning disarmingly. At first, I couldn't believe my eyes. Was it possible, I pondered, that this diminutive person was the Elijah Muhammad, the leader and teacher of America since the death of El-Hajj Malik El-Shabazz, the most powerful Black man since Marcus Garvey and certainly the most mysterious religious leader in the world? He did not look quite as frail as I had been

106

led to believe, but he did cough a bit. Dressed as if to fit his publicity photo, he was indeed a "man in his mid-sixties, 5 feet 6 inches high, scaling the modest weight of 150 pounds." Negro-brown and bald, he wore his famed dark suit and bow tie. It seemed so silly to introduce myself in return, even if formally, for I had the uncanny feeling that he knew every move I had made from the moment I set foot in Chicago.

In an atmosphere of profound quiet, he led me into an inner dining-room where members of his household were waiting, all seated at table in sepulchral silence, waiting for our entrance. It was most dramatic. I must confess that I found this the most unnerving moment of my American experiençe, but once the Messenger began to talk, he had a way of drawing me so completely into his power and presence that, converted or not, I was soon to become conscious of nothing else in the world except a universe trained between Allah and "the blue-eyed devil."

Then came the introduction of his household. At one table in the corner sat his secretaries, looking very beautiful in their ankle-reaching dresses. There were usually four of them, he explained, but one was indisposed and in bed. It was to this team of four secretaries that he dictated his daily letters, speeches, newspaper articles and special messages, from the breakfast table at 7:30 in the morning till late at night. On our own table, Mr. Muhammad himself naturally was at the head, having beckoned me to sit at the other end, facing him. On his immediate right was his wife; and next to her, nearest to me, was the Principal of the University of Islam, the lady who had replaced Sister X, the author of "Muhammad's Children." (Sister Christine left the Muslims with Malcolm X during the Great Split.) On the Messenger's immediate left was John Ali, and next to him was another Muslim "Brother" who kept nudging and urging me in whispers all through the dinner to fire every question I had at the old man because this was my "great chance to get the truth from the horse's mouth." I did. But my conversation with Elijah, the study and analysis of the Muslim Philosophy and Elijah's place in the history of Black Revolution is a subject which deserves a book of its own.

I was deeply concerned at this time with a new revolutionary force which was sweeping America like a tropical fire. It was a force I could understand very well, for that same fire had been burning in my own soul long before I discovered it was common to Black youth of my generation all over the world. Frustration is compelling us all, wherever we are born, to rethink our position.

All men are born free. It is men who make slaves of other men. It is therefore absurd as the generations before us have done, to talk about making people free. You can only talk about stopping oppression. There is no such thing as the abolition of Slavery. You can only talk about destruction of Masterhood. There is no such thing as the Negro problem. What we should be talking about is the White problem. We should be talking about the nuisance-value of a race of people who, because of an illusion about the colour of their skin, are determined by words and deeds to subject the rest of mankind to economic, cultural and political dependency and slavery. And talking about it is not enough either. Because, according to an old Chinese proverb, "the wind of words alone cannot turn the mill of history."

For too many years, Black people in different parts of the world have been suffering at the hands of Whites in what they believe to be isolated pockets of oppression. Hence the Black peoples of Britain think that the Black man's problem will be over once Brixton, Paddington and Perry Bar are "integrated." Hence, the African in Nigeria once thought that "Independence" for his country meant that the Black man could live in freedom. Hence, the Indian worker in Bombay once believed that the problem of the Black man in the Caribbean was different from his own. Hence, millions of Africans in Southern Africa sincerely believe that it is only a handful of White settlers who are keeping them down and actually expect the White men of Britain to come to their aid. Hence, the Afro-

108

American of Detroit thought, until recently, that his White oppressor was a different man from the White oppressor of the Vietnamese people ....

Today we know differently, of course. We know that, in spite of the threadbare old strategy of divide-and-conquer practised by Whites, Black peoples all over the world, wherever they are born, wherever they go, drink the same waters of affliction from the hands of the same man: the White man. We know that the Negro of Harlem in New York has much more in common with the African in Angola than he has with his White neighbour in Manhattan. We know that the attitude of White people to the Blacks all over the world is the same. We know that in America, Black people are being lynched by Anglo-Saxon fascists, and that in Canada, Anglo-Saxon fascism has crystallised into European Preferential Migration and the Anti-Asiatic Act. We know that in Australia Anglo-Saxon civilisation has typically enshrined itself as the White Australia Policy, and that in South Africa, it has escalated to the dizzy heights of Apartheid. We know that in Rhodesia, Anglo-Saxon fascism is rearing its head as UDI, and that the White world, in spite of the lip-deep pious protestations of kith-and-kin statesmen, is applauding the "rebel" Smith regime.

While we see that when we pinpoint the areas of the world's most brutal and despicable racisms today, they coincide with the Anglo-Saxon dispersion. We also know that, on an individual level, the only difference between the Ian Smiths and Harold Wilsons of the White world is not a difference in principle, but a difference in tactics. We know they are both agreed that the African is an inferior being incapable of administering his own community. The only difference is that while the Smiths say this is a permanent impairment, the Wilsons, for pragmatic reasons, say that in time the White man's kiss-of-life might possibly wake up the African and start him developing from his present state of being three-quarters human to a state where he becomes a European who just looks like an

109

African. We know that the quarrel between the Smiths and Wilsons is not a quarrel between fascism and anti-fascism, but a quarrel between frankness and hypocrisy within a fascist framework.

In a word, the Black peoples of the world have found out that what they are facing today is not, as they were once told, isolated pockets of White oppression, but International White Power. And that, isolated, the Black men are weak, and unable to fight from their minority position. But united, they are strong and very much in the majority.

Yet majority without action is impotent. This Black impotency has been exploited by the enemies of the Black people too often, too long, too ruthlessly. What Black people need as a guide for action is a revolutionary philosophy which will educate them to be not only reactive, but also active, a philosophy which must teach the Black man, especially the Uncle Tom who giggles when it doesn't tickle and scratches where it doesn't itch, that man, as Frantz Fanon pointed out, is not only YES, . . . yes to life, yes to love, yes to generosity, but also that man is equally NO, . . . no to scorn, no to degradation, no to exploitation, no to the butchery of what is most human in man: freedom. This philosophy the new Negro of America has begun to call Black Power.

Black Power. I found from experience that, to appreciate the true definition of Black Power, one must first negate the negative definitions of the sensational press. Black Power is not "undefinable." It is not a slogan of dissident Blacks. It is not Black fascism.It does not mean the demand of every White head on a platter. It does not even mean Black domination of the world. To understand the true meaning of the concept of Black Power and how it came about at a certain stage in the psychological dialectic of the American Negro, it is best to take the two words, Black and Power, separately.

Black. For centuries, the Black man in America has chased after a mirage. This mirage he has called integration. It is a mirage because America is traditionally a segregated Society. De facto America consists of Irish quarters,

110

Jewish quarters, German quarters, and as many other quarters as Europe has tribes. There are China towns in San Francisco and New York. There is the Amish intercourse of Pennsylvania. The ghettos where the Negroes are packed in animalistic isolation are well known. Puerto Ricans inevitably live in segregated communities. Even the country's oldest-settler, the American Indian, is not yet integrated into White society. It is therefore unrealistic for the Negro to seek integration in a society so obviously segregated by tradition.

But there was a reason why the Negro not only sought this "integration" but was, in fact, the only racial group that wanted it so intensely. One of the saddest consequences of Negro history is that, while every other racial group in America enjoys a cultural linkage with her past, the Negro was brutally and suddenly cut off from his own. And, not unnaturally, the Negro was obliged to turn to the society of his White master for cultural sustenance and " integration." But the door of White society was slammed in his face. He was segregated. He was lynched. He was frozen out and thrown into the ghetto to stiffle in cultural frustration.

Contrary to White expectation, this became for the Negro a blessing in disguise. The cultural rebuff of the Whites galvanised him into a desperate quest for his past. And the emergence of New African nations, in his land of origin, brought to the open very telling historical facts about his past. Africa was never a cultural vacuum as alleged by Whites. The Negro, realised he has been the victim of a lie and that White cultural superiority is only a White-fabricated tale to dupe the Black man and to provide an excuse for dehumanising the rest of mankind. He sees that "White = Beautiful" and "Black = Ugly and Evil" are untrue equations, morally, culturally, historically; their purpose has only been to convert materials connected with White values and culture into commodities which are exchangeable with the raw materials of those other lands which the White man covets.

Suddenly, the Negro is no longer the Black American

111

ashamed of any identification with his African past; he becomes a hyphenated American, the Afro-American. This has signalled the birth of Negro cultural nationalism in America and, with it, the Negro's rediscovery of Africa. The Negro woman no longer burns her hair to "Whiten" it, aping White values as those Japanese women do who operate on their eyes to cut them into round "White" shapes. Instead of the I-used-to-be-a-Negro straight hair-dos, the Black woman is now beginning to wear the "Natural Hair Style" with pride. Afro-American schools of culture have sprung up everywhere like mushrooms and the Negro has been teaching himself Swahili and other African languages with ardour. In New York and Washing-on, DC, l'Africana Fabio has written fiery poetry about the Burning Spears of Africa. In Atlanta, Georgia, as well as in Watts, culture-voracious SNCC youths have been chanting "Oginga Odinga" with love.

In Chicago, Phillip Cohran, having electrified African musical instruments and given weekly performances at the Harper Theatre, staggered the White world when he declared that White classical music was "unnatural" and profane, and he proceeded to invent his Originalist musical philosophy to prove his case.

All over America, Toms with the House-Nigger mentality have fast reached the autumn of their days and the tide of Black cultural nationalism has been sweeping a new generation of Carmichaels to the fore. From now onwards, Black in Black Power has come to mean for this new generation of Afro-Americans that "our nose is broad, our lips thick, our skin black, and we are beautiful."

Power. Black cultural nationalism without economic power is a sham. And under the present world system where the line of Colour has coincided with the line of Class, no Black man in his right mind can be expected to carry innocence to the point of believing he can seek and get this power within the existing White camp. To seek economic power within this White social structure could only mean a replacement of exploitation of Black by Black,

112

a mere displacement of colour discrimination by class discrimination.

Since the objective is the annihilation of oppression, not the butchery of colour, this would be unsuitable. The only way the Black man can get real power is by smashing the system that incubates exploitation of the Black. If he cannot smash this system from within, he must set in motion an international revolutionary force which will do so from without. The Black man must either smash that system or the system will take advantage of his docility and smash him.

From the foregoing analysis of the two words, Black and Power, one can summarily define Black Power as the totality of the economic, cultural, political and, if necessary, military power which the Black people of the world need to abolish White oppression.

The American that I saw represents the epitome of this White oppression.

It will perhaps surprise some people that, after touring the length and breadth of the United States during what must have been the "hottest" summer in American experience, after wading through the riotous couldron of the North and penetrating the Klan-ridden hell of the South, after meeting the men and women who allegedly make America tick and the teeming masses who, like me, have become victims of that ticking, after conferring with Congressmen and Senators in Washington, DC (Big Deal!), and then being a guest-of-honour the Messenger of Allah himself in Southside Chicago, after seeing the beauty and beauties of New Mexico and the ugliest ugliness of the inside of the Indian Reservation, it will perhaps surprise some people that, after all these moving experiences, I have here pushed masses and masses of these "worthier" materials to the periphery to make a central issue of Dolores, a little black prostitute from Harlem.

I hope this does not surprise you too, my dear beautiful sister, Dolores. For this sort of thing only surprises those people to whom the dignity of man means nothing, and the

113

dignity of woman even less. Even if all this long talk in this long letter means nothing else to you, I want you to understand that I care. If you can understand and accept that, I promise you that, even behind bars in this heart of Babylon, I will feel good inside my heart.

I care. I did what I did because I care. I care deeply, I care. I stopped myself from having you cheaply because I care. I refused to denigrate you, Black mother, even if it meant throwing you out of my hotel room for that same reason. I care. Oh my God, I care. I care because I love you. I love you because you are my sister. You are my sister because — what else could you be but my sister?

All sorts of things went through my head in that hotel room. In that fraction of a second, the tragic history that is yours and mine reeled through my head like a silent film. I asked myself all sorts of questions concerning you, me, and Man. And everytime, I came back to the same nagging paramount question. How could I prove that you were not really my sister?

In my little village in Africa, we have a great tradition of the extended family. I asked myself whether this Black girl I was about to dive into was not really my blood sister? How could I be sure that I was not about to graft my penis into the black xylem of my family tree?

There was only one way I could have told that. And that was by the language you spoke. But you no longer speak a Black tongue today because of the cruel and brutal consequences of slave history.

In those days, it was against the slave law for Black slaves to speak their native tongues. Those who defied this law were known to have been shot on the spot or, it still in transit, thrown into the sea alive to be devoured by sharks. That was how you, my dear Black sister, were stripped of your language, your culture, your dignity, your pride and, inevitably, your human rights. You are the end product of a macabre history which saw the kidnapping and forced transportation of fifty million Black men and women from Africa to the Western slave-plantation within two hundred

114

years. Yours was the background of a history in which a legitimate reign of terror was the only way to converting human beings into beasts of burden by professional "slave breakers." Those who were wounded had ashes, salt and cinders poured into their wounds. Many were castrated and mutilated, some had their ears notched or chopped off, others were burned, roasted alive or simply packed with gun-powder and blown up. The not so lucky were oiled and salted and then fed alive to insects. So satanic did this sort of practice become that the twenty per cent of the slave population who died annually on passage were considered, when all was said and done, the luckiest of the slaves.

Women slaves got the worst of the brunt. They were raped, brutalised, and dehumanised in unspeakable ways. They were not even spared the ordeal of lynching. Cases were numerous where unborn babies slid off the wombs of pregnant women dangling on lynch trees. And as these babies fell to the ground, the rabid lynch mobs rushed forward with sadistic glee to dance over and trample the little infant to a pulpy death. This was excusable because it was considered cheaper to buy a new slave from Africa than to waste the White master's money and time rearing up a baby slave from infancy to adulthood.

These incidents were neither rare nor isolated but indeed a fundamental and integral part of the slave hustle. So frequent did they become, so profitable did the slave master find this cruel hustling of Black flesh, and so despicable did the slave find his condition that instances were many when slaves committed suicide, not to escape suffering, but just to spite their masters. Such, my dear Black sister, is the heritage of Black living death you have borne through no fault of your own. You are a genuine article of the Black Harlem I saw, typical of many Black men and women who, though delivered stillborn into a cruel environment, still go on walking. They have done this to you.

Yet this is not the end of the story. For, right now in my mind's eye, I can still see you as you were that night in that

115

hotel room. Stripped to the last public fibre of your dignity, you were grovelling on your knees like a little slave woman, taking off the shoes of your purchaser, and getting all set to engulf his urinary pipe in your mouth, re-enacting that macabre history all over again.

But there was a difference this time though. And it wasn't slight. The ruthless slave purchaser was no longer the White man. Certainly not that night in the hotel room. The Black man had taken over where the White man had left off. This was the role in which I saw myself that night. In one fleeting fraction of a second, I had looked into the long mirror by the bedside and had seen myself standing there, undoing my buttons like a lusty slave-breaker, while you, like a choiceless Black slave-woman of old, were on your knees, getting ready to zip down my pants and bury your head in my lap, like a helpless little lamb sucking its mother. I felt so sick with myself that I couldn't stand the scene a moment longer. I never felt so uptight in my life. That was why I leaped back so suddenly land ordered you to quit and split.

I was not angry with you. I was angry with myself. Contrary to what you thought, it was not the nakedness of your body that sickened me. At that precise moment, it was the nakedness of my soul. I repeat without hesitation what I said at the beginning of this letter. You are the most beautiful woman I have ever seen in the nude. I would like to say a lot more but I can't. They censor our letters here. The worst thing about prison is not being allowed to make decisions. But don't grieve for me. I have long come to the conclusion that the Black man has no right to live like a man till he learns to die like a man. Bernard Shaw once wrote that history is full of examples of men and women who have embraced death to avoid destruction.

I remember an article I read a few weeks ago. It told a sad little story about a Vietcong girl who had been killed in battle. A love letter found on her body revealed how lonely she had been for a man she knew she might never see again. She had loved him deeply and yet left him behind to go into

116

the jungle to die for her convictions. Her letter contained the saddest line a woman ever wrote to her man: "When my little lamp goes out, I hold your shadow in my arms."

You couldn't with anyone a nobler death, male or female. I can now hear the rattling of keys and footsteps on the landing. That means the warders are coming to switch off the light for the night. I cannot promise to hold your shadow in my arms, having failed you once as a lover, but I do promise that from now till my dying day, I will never cease thinking of you as a sister among sisters. Goodnight.

Your brother,

OBI.

www.ingramcontent.com/pod-product-compliance
Lightning Source LLC
Chambersburg PA
CBHW010253030726
47497CB00010BA/3197